HOME FOR THE HOLLY DAYS

CINDY KIRK

WAVERLY
HOUSE

ISBN: 9798502257114

CHAPTER ONE

Krista Ankrom gazed out the restaurant's ninth-floor window at the festive scene below. The Norway spruce decorated for Christmas stood tall and majestic in Rockefeller Center. The splendor of its 50,000 LED lights was surpassed only by the Swarovski star at the top. Krista remembered a news anchor mentioning yesterday at the tree lighting that the star was covered with three million crystals.

The gorgeous scene should have buoyed her flagging spirits, as should this impromptu lunch with her friend.

Across the table, Desz Presley answered work emails and sipped her drink. It was a given that when she and Desz visited L'Avenue for lunch, her friend would multitask while enjoying sea bass and an Aperol Spritz.

Krista returned her attention to the tree covered in multicolored lights, the throngs of tourists skating in front of it, and the Salvation Army Santa on the corner. An engaging scene straight out of a Hallmark movie. Most years, she lovingly drank it in.

"Krista? Are you listening?"

"Hmmm? What? Sorry, Desz. I spaced out watching the

skaters." Krista waved an airy hand, not wanting to burden her friend with her thoughts.

"What, you mean you weren't riveted by me complaining about my parents again?"

Though Desz had fully embraced life in NYC since moving here three years ago, at Christmas she loved going home to Tennessee and her family's lavish Christmas celebrations. This year, Desz's parents had opted for a cruise, leaving Desz to spend Christmas in the city.

"I know how you feel." Krista pulled her gaze from the window to give her friend her full attention. "I hoped my family would come spend Christmas with me this year. But Tom and his wife just had their first child, and traveling with a baby can be difficult."

Desz took another sip of her drink. "Remind me why you aren't going there?"

"I considered it until I learned Claire's parents are also spending the holidays with them. It'll be a full house." Krista lifted her glass of spring water. "It figures the one year I'm free, enjoying a family Christmas isn't an option."

"You've always worked over the holidays." Desz sipped her drink, a thoughtful look creasing her brow. "Or you have every year since we first met."

"I planned to get the Japan job and be in Tokyo this month. Not meant to be." Krista had known the repeatedly delayed contract offer had been a bad sign. It didn't matter what her agent, Merline, said about age being no cause for concern, at twenty-eight, Krista understood the realities of her situation.

She'd been right to be concerned. The model chosen to be the new face of Shibusa Cosmetics was a decade younger than she was.

"You'll get another account. A bigger, better one." Desz's voice rang with confidence. "Shibusa will regret not choosing you."

Krista lifted her water in a toast. "I'll drink to that."

Her mocking tone had Desz chuckling before she changed the subject. "At least your parents are staying home to spend Christmas with their first grandchild. My parents are choosing a seafood buffet on the lido deck over me. In what world is that tradition?"

Krista laughed. "No more than working over the holidays can be considered a tradition."

"I'd say you're due for a change." Desz's dark eyes sparkled. "You're an independent woman with enough money to do whatever you want. You should go somewhere. Hey, what am I saying? *We* should go somewhere. Where do you want to go? Totally your call."

An image of the quaint community she'd loved near the Canadian border flashed in Krista's mind. "It's not a place you'd be interested in."

Desz leaned forward. "You let me decide."

"Holly Pointe." Simply saying the name brought a smile to Krista's lips. "Before I got my first big modeling contract and moved to New York, my family spent every Christmas in Vermont."

"Holly Pointe, Vermont." Desz rolled the name around on her tongue, then smiled. "I've never been that far north."

"It's lovely there." Krista sighed. "A picture postcard of how life can be."

Desz cocked her head. "Huh?"

"People in Holly Pointe care about one another. Everyone takes time to enjoy the holidays." Krista smiled, remembering all the events. "There's always a big tree lighting, followed by caroling in the town square. Santa is, well, everywhere. All the buildings are decorated and—"

Krista stopped herself, recalling the elaborate traditions Desz had told her about in Nashville. "It's very humble compared to the Christmas celebrations you're used to."

"It sounds fabulous." Desz clasped her hands together. "I've never experienced a small-town Christmas."

It almost sounded as if Desz was open to going to Holly Pointe. Krista's smile grew. If she couldn't be with her family at Christmas, maybe being in a place that reminded her of them would be the next best thing.

"Does going there for several weeks sound like something you'd want to do?" Krista knew Desz could work from anywhere, and a few weeks someplace free of billboards and ad agencies might help her stop stressing about work.

"I can be packed and ready to leave tomorrow morning."

For the first time since learning she hadn't gotten the Shibusa account, Krista experienced a surge of holiday happiness. She lifted her glass. "To the best Christmas ever."

Desz clinked her glass against Krista's. "To new adventures."

Dustin Bellamy strode down Fifth Avenue, a man on a mission. Out of the corner of his eye, he saw a guy burst out of a store and barrel his way toward the curb where a cab had just pulled up.

The man brushed past him, would have clipped him, if Dustin's reflexes hadn't been good. Built like a bull, the guy reminded Dustin of Stan, a teammate. Stan with his hard wrist shot and a willingness to drop the gloves.

God, he missed his friends. Even the hot-tempered ones.

Lost in thought for several seconds, Dustin stood there while the crowd parted around him. Then he began walking, not wanting to keep the doctor waiting. Though Dustin had to sprint the last two blocks, he stepped off the elevator on the fifth floor with three minutes to spare.

The receptionist, an attractive woman with blonde hair, stood when Dustin entered.

"I'm Dustin Bellamy," he told her. "I have an appointment with Dr. Wallace."

"I know who you are," she said with a smile. "Let me show you the way."

Instead of an exam room, she ushered him into the doctor's luxurious private office.

She inclined her head. "May I get you something to drink while you wait?"

Dustin shook his head. "I'm fine. Thanks."

"The doctor should only be a few minutes." With the promise hanging in the air, she pulled the door closed behind her.

Restless, Dustin wandered the spacious area with its huge flat-screen TV and a standing desk in walnut. A wall of shelves near a sitting area held not only books, but medical awards and several modern sculptures of athletes.

Eric Wallace, orthopedic surgeon and sports medicine guru, had come highly recommended. Though only in his late forties, he was the team physician for several professional sports teams as well as numerous top athletes.

Dustin moved to the window and glanced down on the busy street below. He turned when he heard the door open, his heart kicking into high gear.

Tall and lean, the doctor moved with the grace of an athlete, holding out a hand as he crossed the last few feet to Dustin.

"Eric Wallace. It's a pleasure to finally meet you, Mr. Bellamy." His hand closed around Dustin's in a firm shake. "I'm a huge fan. Please, have a seat."

The doctor gestured to an area with several chairs and a small sofa. Dustin chose one, and the doctor sat in another opposite his.

After a few minutes of polite conversation, Dr. Wallace got down to business. "I reviewed your records and the most recent MRI. You're aware that normally the ACL tears when the muscles around the knee are weak. Because of all the skating you do, that isn't the case with you, not in regard to your previous injury or with this most recent one. Your tests show the muscles around your knee are well-developed and strong. But hockey puts a lot of stress on the ligament due to the twisting, pivoting and cutting."

"The original tear was from a collision with another player," Dustin offered, though the information was in the records.

Wallace nodded. "After the first injury, it appears you had excellent surgical results from the tendon graft."

"I worked hard at rehab." Dustin kept his attention on the doctor's face, searching for the slightest hint of encouragement. "After seven months of intense work, I was back to a hundred percent when I returned to the ice."

The doctor nodded, his expression softening. "I watched the game where you were checked. You kept playing despite rein-juring the ligament."

"It was the first game of the finals." Dustin lifted his chin to meet the doctor's questioning gaze head on. "The trainers braced the knee."

"I'm sure you were aware that playing with a damaged ACL opened you up to further injury." The doctor spoke in a matter-of-fact tone.

"My team needed me. We were in the playoffs." Dustin's breathing wanted to spike, but he kept it slow and easy. "I have no regrets. Winning the Cup was worth it. Since June, I've worked on staying fit and healthy. I can skate, but it's clear that without surgery I won't be able to get back to a competitive level."

Dr. Wallace sat back in his chair, regret blanketing his face. "I'm sorry, Dustin. I can't recommend another surgery."

"I don't think you understand. I'm willing—eager—to do whatever it takes." Dustin leaned forward. "What about platelet-rich plasma treatments to speed healing? I know you've used it on hockey players."

"PRP treatments can speed healing and stimulate tissue regeneration in the treated area after surgery. However, as I stated, I can't recommend a second ACL surgical intervention for you." Compassion filled the doctor's blue eyes. "Not based on the extent of your injury."

Dustin had to stop himself from jumping up and railing at the doctor. Didn't the man understand? Hockey was more than a game to him. It was his life.

Over the years, Dustin had become an expert at pushing past the pain. Most of the time, it was physical. Hockey—at any level, but especially at the highest level—was hard on the body. It also demanded a mental toughness.

Cultivating that toughness paid off now as he kept his expression impassive, showing no reaction to the news.

"I realize this isn't what you hoped to hear." The doctor's voice gentled. "I concur with your team specialist and the other physician you saw that the second injury to your ACL and playing while injured contributed to what we're seeing on the MRI. Surgery is not advised and, if done, would not give you the desired results."

Dustin had heard it all before. Still, he'd held out hope.

"Is there a chance you're wrong?" Dustin had never been one to give up easily. That tenacity and determination had served him well over the years. "Like I said, I'm willing to put in the work, do whatever—"

"I'm not wrong." Despite the firm tone, sympathy filled the doctor's pale blue eyes. "The fact that you've worked so hard on your rehab after the first surgery is why you were able to go back. Continuing to play after sustaining the second injury was a game changer."

As much as he wanted to return to his team, Dustin wouldn't go back and be less. His teammates, who wanted to win, deserved better.

Pushing to his feet, Dustin stuck out his hand. "I appreciate your time."

The doctor rose and gave his hand a firm shake. "You were an amazing player."

Were. Even the doctor was speaking in the past tense.

Dustin rode the elevator down to the main floor of the midtown office building, disappointment and grief battering at his control.

Helping his team win the Stanley Cup had been worth it, he reminded himself. Despite the positive thoughts, when he stepped outside, Dustin had to stop to catch his breath.

Hockey had been his life. The other players, his family. All that was gone now.

The irritating buzz of his phone had him setting his jaw in a hard line. If some reporter had gotten his private number...

Dustin jerked the phone from his pocket and glanced at the display. He took a steadying breath before he answered. "Hi, Dad."

"How did the doctor's visit go?" The carefully cultivated easy tone didn't fool Dustin. His father was as apprehensive about this visit as he'd been.

"Wallace concurs with the other two."

Silence for one, two, three long seconds.

"Perhaps there's someone else. I heard of a doctor in—"

"Dad. This guy was thorough." Dustin kept his tone matter-of-fact, understanding this news was nearly as devastating to his father as it was to him.

Hockey hadn't just been Dustin's life for the past twenty-plus years, starting with peewee leagues, it had been his father's life, as well.

"I'm sorry, son." Terry Bellamy cleared his throat, then spoke in a light tone. "What are you going to do? You are the Player with the Plan, after all."

The moniker the media had given Dustin early in his career

had stuck. He'd not only been a physical player, but he'd managed his emotions and kept his focus. He'd played smart. Not only on the ice, but in how he'd managed his career.

The six-year multimillion-dollar contract he'd signed shortly before his first injury had been one of the smartest.

"I'm considering several possibilities. Freddie and I will be discussing all my options in more depth."

His dad didn't push. From the time he'd been drafted at twenty-two, Dustin had been in charge of his career. With, of course, input from his agent, Freddie Wurtz.

"Your mom and I would love to have you home this Christmas."

"I have no doubt Ashleigh's boys will keep you both extremely busy." Dustin's sister had four kids under eight. His mom and dad doted on their grandsons.

"They'd love to see Uncle Dustin." His dad's tone turned persuasive. He obviously was not ready to give up without a fight.

Dustin had no doubt some of his tenacity came from this man, who'd been such a strong support all these years.

Which was why Dustin knew he needed a good reason not to go to Minnesota and spend Christmas with the family. Not wanting to deal with questions about his future wouldn't be considered an acceptable excuse.

"There's this woman I've been seeing." Dustin kept his tone casual. "I'm going to spend the holidays with her."

"Oh. Really?" His dad's voice held surprise. "You haven't mentioned anyone. You always said hockey and relationships are impossible together."

"That's what I thought." Dustin hadn't mentioned anyone, because there was no one to mention. But he couldn't deal with the family right now, so fictional girlfriend it was. "Thanks for all you've done, Dad. I couldn't have made it this far without you."

"You sound as if your life is over." Worry filled his dad's voice. "This is simply the beginning of a new chapter."

"It is." Dustin spoke with more confidence than he felt at the moment. "We'll talk later."

No longer the Player with the Plan, Dustin began walking and soon found himself at Rockefeller Center, gazing down at the skaters going around and around on the ice.

The tree and other signs of the approaching holiday season seemed a mockery of the sadness that held him in a stranglehold.

What am I going to do?

The grip on his chest tightened at the question.

He pulled out his phone, then realized he had no one to call. His best friends were also his teammates, and he wasn't ready to talk to them about this. Regardless of what he'd said to his dad, he also didn't want to deal with his agent. Not yet. And he couldn't call a girlfriend who didn't exist.

In this city of millions, Dustin suddenly felt very alone. His lavish hotel suite held no appeal. Besides, when he'd slipped out of the hotel this morning, he'd noticed a couple of sports reporters in the lobby.

He needed a place to lie low. A place to regroup. Most of all, a place that would give him the time and space necessary to come up with a plan.

CHAPTER TWO

The day after their luncheon at L'Avenue, Krista and Desz left New York City for Vermont in a rented cherry-red Subaru. Snow-packed highways, plus a couple of wrecks due to ice on the roads, made for a white-knuckled trip.

Krista pulled the car to a stop in front of the cabin, thankful they hadn't needed to make another stop. According to the caretaker, the key would be waiting for them under the front mat. Krista released her death grip on the steering wheel and sat back. "Finally."

"It went quickly." Despite the fact that a normally seven- hour trip had taken ten, Desz's smile came readily. "Chatting with you made time fly."

Desz leaned forward in her seat. Brown eyes snapped with excitement as she took in the log cabin's spacious front porch and high-pitched metal roof. She smiled at the sight of the evergreen wreath with the big red bow on the door.

"When you said rustic, I pictured a hunting cabin." Desz released her seat belt and shifted to face Krista. "This place is lovely and lots bigger than I expected."

Krista pushed open her car door. "It housed our family of four comfortably."

"I like space." Desz expelled a satisfied breath. "I'm going to enjoy spreading out."

Once they reached the porch, Krista reached under the mat and grabbed the key.

"I wondered how we were going to get in." Amusement filled Desz's voice. "Appears no one around here is worried about a break-in."

Krista unlocked the door and flipped on the lights before turning back to Desz. "Technically, it wouldn't be a break-in if they had the key."

"Good point."

Warm air greeted Krista as she moved farther inside the cabin. "This was nice of her."

"Who?" Desz paused in her perusal of the room.

"Maggi, the caretaker, upped the heat. They usually keep the temp low when a cabin is unoccupied." The thoughtfulness of the gesture squeezed Krista's heart. "That's why it's already comfortable in here."

"I don't know Maggi, but I like her already." Desz lowered the backpack slung over her shoulder onto the sofa.

"Perhaps things haven't changed that much here," Krista murmured.

"Quit worrying." Reaching over, Desz gave Krista's arm a playful squeeze before doing a three-sixty. "It'll be great."

Krista watched her friend's approving gaze linger on the stone fireplace and the flat-screen television before shifting to the fully equipped kitchen with its honey-colored cabinets.

A bar counter between the kitchen and the rustic farmhouse table practically begged a cold and weary traveler to sit on one of the stools and enjoy a cup of hot cocoa.

Krista pointed. "My brother and I used to eat Christmas cookies at that counter."

"I'm glad you were able to get this cabin," Desz told her. "It sounds like these walls hold a lot of terrific memories."

Krista nodded. She'd been shocked to discover the cabin, the one they'd rented every year and considered the family cabin, would be unoccupied until the end of the year. Back in the day, her parents had needed to book a year in advance.

"It has a good vibe." Desz gave a decisive nod as she continued to explore.

"It does," Krista agreed.

Desz's gaze shifted upward to the cathedral ceiling with its lovely exposed beams, then to the stairs leading up to the second level.

"There are two bedrooms up there and a full bath between them. That's where Tom and I slept," Krista explained.

Desz cocked her head. "What about your parents?"

Krista gestured to a door off the living area. "There's a bedroom and bath through there."

Desz gave an approving nod. "Nice...and private. I bet they liked that."

"I never thought about them needing privacy." Just the thought made Krista twitchy.

Shifting her attention to the space in front of the picture window, Desz gestured with her head. "I bet that's where the tree went every year. Right in front of the window. Am I right?"

"You guessed it." Krista found her lips curving as more fond memories flooded back. "Shortly after we arrived, we'd head out to pick our tree. My mom loves Christmas. She'd go crazy with decorations."

"You want to hear Christmas crazy?" Desz gave a little laugh. "My parents had seven professionally decorated trees in their house last year. Seven. I'm going to miss that."

Hearing the wistful quality in Desz's voice, Krista plunged ahead. "There's no reason we can't have a tree. Or more than one."

"I'd be okay with one," Desz said, then quickly added, "As long as we go crazy with decorations."

Krista lifted her hands, palms up. "Is there any other way?"

"Not in my world." Desz's droll tone had Krista laughing as her friend strode across the room.

Picking up a carved wooden moose from the mantel, she turned it in her hand. "The workmanship on this is amazing."

Crossing the room, Krista leaned close. "Look at the detail on the antlers."

"I'd love to interview the person who did this for my blog." Seeing Krista's look of surprise, Desz continued. "My dad said I was born with the curiosity gene. I've always been curious about, well, about most everything. I loved to hang around when the designers came to decorate our trees so they could give me tips."

After returning the moose to its spot on the mantel, Desz turned to Krista and shook her head. "I can't imagine being away from this place for ten years."

Krista shrugged. "Life happened."

"Now, here you are, back where you started."

She knew Desz hadn't meant the comment the way Krista took it, but in many ways, it felt as if she was on the verge of starting over. This time with no idea where she was headed.

Unzipping her backpack, Desz surprised Krista by producing a bottle of wine. "Why don't you round up a couple of glasses? We'll toast our arrival."

"Put that away," Krista joked, gesturing to the bottle Desz held. "I bought a bottle of Cristal a couple of weeks ago. I should have brought it with me."

"Ah, yes, you definitely should have. This wine is good, but I love Cristal."

"Me, too." Krista's lips lifted in a rueful smile. "I planned to open the bottle when the Shibusa deal came through."

Desz offered an encouraging smile. "Speed bump."

Krista pulled two wineglasses from the cupboard. She wanted to agree, but couldn't. "More like hitting a brick wall."

Looking back, Krista wasn't sure what had been worse. Getting the news from her agent or seeing the worry in Merline's eyes.

"You're strong and resilient. You'll push through that brick wall like it's made of marshmallows." Desz cocked her head and stared at the glasses in Krista's hands. "I know we're roughing it, but please don't tell me you expect me to open this bottle with my teeth."

Krista rolled her eyes, but chuckled as she returned to the kitchen for a corkscrew.

Minutes later, she and Desz sat on the sofa, each with a glass of wine in hand. A fire, now dancing merrily in the hearth, added a golden glow to the room.

Taking a sip of wine, Desz glanced around the living area. "I believe Holly Pointe will provide excellent fodder for my blog."

"How's it going, by the way?"

Desz arched a questioning brow.

"The blog." Krista offered an embarrassed chuckle. "We've spent so much time talking about me, I haven't asked about you."

"You're forgiven." Desz relaxed against the overstuffed sofa. "It's going remarkably well. Readership is way up. Just this week, I secured a couple more sponsors. Still, my goal while I'm here is to start considering the future."

Krista took a sip of her wine. "What do you mean? If it's going well, what is it that you'd want to change?"

"Nothing right now. The thing is, the cyberworld is constantly evolving. While blogs are hot right now, I want to keep my eyes open for the next latest and greatest so I can be ready to pivot."

Krista stared at her friend in admiration. "You're so—"

"Ambitious?" Desz smiled. "I'd say it takes one to know one."

She clinked her wineglass against Krista's.

Krista rested her head against the back of the sofa, but couldn't relax. She straightened, gesturing with her hands. "I don't feel ambitious right now. I feel like I don't have control over anything. Merline doesn't anticipate having trouble booking me for other shoots. Just not the big accounts."

"That's crazy! If Merline can't get you the accounts you deserve, you'll find a new agent who can."

Krista loved her friend's loyalty, even if her take on the industry was not exactly accurate.

"Easy, Desz. Merline is in my corner, always has been. But the writing is on the wall." Krista wanted to stay positive, but she'd been in the business long enough to be realistic. She forced a smile. "Fortunately, I have a great example to follow."

Desz raised her eyebrows and paused midsip.

"Like you, I'm going to focus on the future and figuring out where I fit." Krista glanced around the cabin. "You were right when you said that coming here is like going back to the beginning for me. I'm hoping the time here will bring clarity. At the very least, we'll have fun. That much, I can guarantee."

"I'm glad you suggested this." The multicolored tassels on the end of Desz's red stocking cap swayed as she bopped down the sidewalks of Holly Pointe. "After those hours in the car, I needed to get out and walk. And I want to get a better look at the town."

"This way, you can see it at night, and we can enjoy an amazing meal without us having to cook." Krista hoped Rosie's was still the place to eat in Holly Pointe. "Rosie's Diner is local. It used to be very popular. I don't know if it still is, or—"

Desz waved a dismissive hand. "Anyplace that's not a chain is fine with me."

"There are no chains in Holly Pointe." Krista gazed at the

businesses lining both sides of the historic downtown district. "That local flavor is what makes this community so special."

Desz's lips curved. "I feel as if I've stepped into an alternate universe."

"A good alternate universe?"

Desz gestured with one hand to the brightly lit business district. "Could something this charming be anything but?"

"Excellent point." Krista paused, letting the sound of Christmas music and the sights of quaint storefronts boasting brightly colored awnings and a plethora of holiday lights wrap around her. Banners in rich reds and greens, touting Holly Days, waved from street poles in the light breeze.

At the far end of the street, the iconic courthouse rose, tall and dignified. Constructed of brick and stone, with rounded arches, endless gingerbread accents and bell towers, the late-nineteenth-century structure looked more like a church than a municipal building.

Colored lights on the front of the building had been strung to proclaim "Happy Holly Days."

Desz cocked her head. "Holly Days?"

"The time before Christmas when all the holiday activities take place," Krista explained.

"The Marketplace you spoke of during the drive here."

"That's just one part of the Holly Days experience."

"Is the Marketplace nearby?" Desz glanced around. "I'd love to see it."

"I believe it opens tomorrow. At least it used to run the three weeks leading up to Christmas." Krista was as eager as Desz to check it out. "The Barns at Grace Hollow, that's where the Marketplace will be set up, were built after my family quit coming here. I can't wait to see them in person."

"It's nice being here through the end of the month." Desz chuckled. "We don't need to cram in everything right away."

As Desz could write her blog from anywhere, and Krista

didn't have any end-of-the-year assignments, they'd booked the cabin through New Year's Day.

Rosie's Diner came into view, its large windows overlooking Main Street encircled in lights that resembled peppermint candies. The glass sported window clings of quirky Christmas gnomes. Greenery interspersed with plaid bows and holly berries added a more traditional touch around the diner's entrance.

Desz pointed to the Grinch pretending to be a gnome with a mug of frothy beer in one hand. She chuckled. "I love Rosie's already."

Then the café door opened, and some serious smells spilled out.

Desz inhaled deeply, and her eyes brightened. "My nose tells me I'm going to love it even more an hour from now."

On Saturday morning, Krista and Desz rose early and headed downtown.

"The Busy Bean is owned by Kenny and Norma Douglas," Krista explained as they approached the front "porch" of the shop. Decorated with hanging oversized ornaments and galvanized buckets of greenery spelling out JOY, the scene offered a warm welcome. "Norma also owns Dough See Dough, the bakery next door. Kenny plays Santa Claus every year."

She'd nearly forgotten that, Krista thought, as she followed Desz into the coffee shop.

The bells over the door jingled. Laughter and conversation filled the air.

"Welcome to the Busy Bean." Kenny called out from behind the counter, even as his attention remained on the couple he was ringing up.

Once he finished, he turned and offered Krista and Desz a broad, welcoming smile.

"What can I get you, ladies? We have—" Kenny stopped, and eyes shadowed by wild, bushy brows widened. "Krista? Krista Ankrom? Is that really you?"

Though she'd recognized Kenny, Krista hadn't expected him to remember her.

"It's me, Mr. Douglas," she told him. "I'm surprised you recognized me."

"Norma and I," he jerked his head in the direction of a rotund woman arranging scones on a pedestal platter, "have followed your career. You're a star."

A falling star.

Krista immediately shoved aside the negative self-talk, reminding herself that a closed door was simply a new opportunity.

Krista smiled at Kenny. "That's kind of you to say."

"It's the truth," Kenny insisted. "And, please, call me Kenny."

"I understand you're Santa Claus." Desz, never one to remain on the sidelines for long, spoke up.

Grateful to her friend for reminding her she had neglected the basic social niceties, Krista made quick work of introductions.

"The Santa Claus thing," Kenny kept his voice low, casting a glance at a family with three small children, "needs to be our little secret."

"I'm sorry," Desz said, instantly contrite.

"No worries." Kenny waved a hand.

His kind smile had Desz's shoulders relaxing.

"How are you enjoying Holly Pointe?"

"We just arrived yesterday," Desz explained. "So far, so wonderful."

"We're happy you came." Norma strode over as she spoke. The jet-black hair Krista remembered was now peppered with gray. A smile, warm and friendly, lifted her generous mouth as she covered the orange and cranberry scones with a glass dome. "Rosie told me you were at her place last night."

Krista saw surprise on Desz's face. Then she remembered her friend didn't grow up in a small town. Desz likely didn't understand how fast news spread in communities like Holly Pointe.

Norma exchanged a glance with her husband before refocusing on the two women. "How long will you be staying?"

"We're here through the holidays," Desz answered. "I can't wait to check out the Marketplace. Krista says that starts today?"

Hearing the question in her voice, Norma confirmed, "It does. Runs right up to Christmas Day." Norma glanced at her husband. "We're hoping for a good turnout."

"I loved Holly Days." Krista smiled at Norma. "I was telling Desz this is a new location for the artisans. From the pictures I've seen, it appears to be an amazing venue."

"The barns are gorgeous and the perfect place to set up out of the weather. We're grateful to Paula Franks for giving us a reduced price on the space." Norma's smile wavered for a second. "We need all the help we can get, what with Holly Days facing increased competition."

An uneasy feeling swept over Krista as she recalled how she'd been able to rent the cabin at the last minute. She barely stopped herself from asking Norma and Kenny if Holly Days was in serious trouble.

When a tour bus pulled up outside and began unloading, Krista's concern decreased. These large buses were always a welcome sight in communities that embraced tourism. Still, she couldn't fail to notice that the crowd exiting the bus wasn't as large as it could have been.

Wanting to beat the line, she and Desz quickly ordered. After collecting their drinks and scones, they settled at a table by the window.

"This shop is darling." Desz took a deep sip of her drink and sighed. "And this peppermint coffee is yummy."

At a nearby table, two guys in their twenties cast interested glances in their direction.

Krista, accustomed to stares and second glances, paid them no attention. She'd learned that even the slightest smile could be seen as encouragement.

Desz, on the other hand, offered the duo a friendly smile before returning her attention to Krista. "Do you know those two?"

"The blond one looks vaguely familiar." Krista shrugged. "I don't recall his name."

"They're staring." Desz spoke in a hushed whisper.

Krista took a long drink, savoring the taste of the spiced chai. "Happens all the time."

"To you maybe," Desz told her. "Not to me."

"Don't give me that." Krista rolled her eyes. "When I first saw you at the agency, I thought for sure you were another model. You looked like you could be Naomi Campbell's little sister. Everyone said so."

Desz laughed. "Flatterer."

"Truth." Krista bit into her scone and chewed. "I never imagined you were a temp."

"I adore our meet-cute story." Desz expelled an exaggerated breath and brought clasped hands to her chest. She dropped her voice to a whisper. "Though maybe you want to save that meet-cute energy for the guys at that table."

Laughing, Krista could only shake her head. Was it any wonder this woman was her best friend?

CHAPTER THREE

Desz looked up from her laptop screen as Krista pulled on her coat. Beside Desz sat a cup of steaming coffee and one of the scones they'd brought back from this morning's visit to the Busy Bean.

After leaving the coffee shop, they'd strolled in and out of the downtown shops. By the time they'd returned to the cabin, it had been time for lunch.

They'd eaten, and when Desz mentioned wanting to get a little work done before they went out again, Krista had picked up the novel she'd brought with her. She'd just opened it when Kenny called.

Krista hadn't asked how he'd gotten her private number. She assumed Maggi had given it to him. Such was the way of small towns.

Desz shifted on the stool at the breakfast bar where she'd set up. "Seriously, if you want me to go with you, I will."

"Stay and get your work done." Krista buttoned her cashmere coat and pulled on her leather gloves. "I'm not sure what Kenny wants, but it shouldn't take long. There will still be plenty of time for us to make it to the barns today."

"No worries. When Santa calls, you gotta answer." Desz cocked her head, and her expression turned thoughtful. "That might make an interesting topic for a blog."

Krista couldn't see how, but if anyone could put a unique spin on the topic, Desz could.

"I can't believe how much Kenny looked like Santa, even without the red suit and hat." Desz's lips curved. "He's got the belly, the long white beard, even the twinkle in his eye."

"Kenny has been playing Santa for as far back as I can remember." Krista shook her head. "What I can't believe is that he's the mayor of Holly Pointe. It's hard for me to picture him in that role."

"The woman at the diner last night—"

"Rose Kelly, the owner," Krista supplied.

"When you went to the restroom, she told me she's on some committee with him to promote Holly Days."

"I hope all their work pays off." Krista pulled her brows together. "I was surprised we didn't see more people in the shops this morning. I hope it's because they're all at the barns for opening day. Or maybe foot traffic picks up closer to Christmas."

"Maybe, but it's also a different world than it was ten years ago." Desz waved a careless hand. "People shop online. They work 24/7. Events their parents loved aren't important to them. You have to be constantly thinking outside of the box, or you're left in the dust."

Which is why, Krista thought, *Desz is so successful.* No grass would dare grow under her feet.

"Well, wish me luck."

"I'm surprised Kenny didn't mention needing to speak with you when we were in this morning."

Desz's comment had Krista turning back, gloved fingers still curved around the doorknob.

"It's a mystery." Krista's ghoulish tone brought a smile to Desz's lips. "The answer shall soon be revealed."

Krista stepped outside to the sound of Desz's laughter. She stood on the porch for a moment, lifting her face to the sun as she breathed in the fresh scent of pine. Instead of driving to the Busy Bean, she decided to walk.

She noticed a Jeep parked in front of the adjacent cabin. She didn't think it had been there yesterday. The cabins were so close she'd have noticed.

Krista made a mental note to keep an eye out for the occupants. If it was a family's first time in Holly Pointe, she would definitely want to make them feel welcome.

For now, she had a mystery to solve.

After arriving in Holly Pointe late last night, Dustin really wasn't in the mood for a chat with the town's mayor. The summons, er, invitation, from Kenny had been relayed to him through Maggi. She'd left a note on the kitchen table that he discovered when he arrived.

Still, with no food or coffee in the cupboards, grabbing something to eat at the Busy Bean held appeal. After his meeting with Kenny, he could grab a few necessities at the food market down the street.

Dustin studied his surroundings as he reached the edge of town. He'd left the rental Jeep he picked up after his plane landed in Burlington back at the cabin, preferring to walk the short distance.

From what he'd observed, at least so far, Holly Pointe hadn't changed much. With everything in his life in turmoil, it was comforting to know that some things were constant.

As he strode down the sidewalk to the coffee shop, he noticed that signs of Christmas were everywhere. That, too, hadn't changed. The only thing different was the scarcity of people. When he'd been a kid, the sidewalks had been crowded with tourists peering in store windows and coming in and out of shops and cafés.

A whiteboard outside the Busy Bean touted peppermint coffee as a special. Dustin grimaced. He'd never been one for flavored brews.

Bells over the door jingled, and a plump woman, her dark hair peppered with gray, turned. Her smile widened when she recognized him. "Come in. Come in."

Dustin closed the distance to the counter in several long strides. He remembered Norma with great fondness. She'd always slipped him and his sister brightly colored Christmas cookies on their way out of her bakery. Their mother must have known—the woman never missed a thing—but when Norma had touched a finger to her lips as if the cookie was their secret, it added to the fun.

Dustin smiled. "It's good to see you again."

"I can say the same." She rounded the counter to give him a hug, then held him at arm's length. "I swear you've grown three inches since I last saw you."

"Probably," he agreed. "I was only seventeen the last time I was here."

Though some boys finished growing at seventeen, Dustin had been destined not to reach his full height until he finished college. Topping out at six feet, one inches had pleased the NHL coaches. Those college years had also given him the chance to grow stronger, ultimately making him more desirable in the draft.

Norma dropped her arms and took a step back. "Having you back, well, like I told Kenny, it's like it was meant to be."

It was an odd remark. As Dustin couldn't think of a response, he simply smiled. "Is Kenny around? I got a message he wanted me to stop by and see him."

"He's in the far corner." Norma gestured with one hand, but when he turned to go, she placed a staying hand on his arm.

"Tell me what you want to drink and eat. I'll bring it to the table."

Dustin glanced at the hanging menu, then ordered coffee—strong and black—and avocado toast. It seemed the healthiest option on the menu.

"I remember how you loved my cookies." Norma patted his arm. "I haven't brought any over here from the bakery yet. When I do, there's a blue star with your name on it."

Laughing, Dustin felt the tension he'd brought with him drop to the floor. Coming to Holly Pointe had been the right move. Here, he could recharge and rethink his future without everyone asking him what he was going to do.

Dustin pulled out several bills to pay, but Norma pushed the money aside.

"On the house." She gestured with her head. "The way my husband is motioning to you tells me he's eager to see you. It'll only be a minute for your order."

"Thanks, Norma." When the older woman turned, Dustin stuffed a wad of bills into the tip jar before focusing on where Kenny sat at a square table in the corner of the dining area. A woman sat with him, her back to Dustin. Even though he couldn't see her face, he guessed she was closer to his age than to Kenny's. One of his daughters perhaps.

Another person at this meeting surprised him, though it really shouldn't since he still didn't have a clue what the mayor wanted with him.

No time like the present to find out.

Crossing the room in several long strides, Dustin pulled up short when the woman at Kenny's table turned toward him.

Not one of Kenny's daughters.

"Krista?"

With her dark hair tousled around her beautiful face, she looked even more lovely than she had in the barrage of pictures he'd seen of her. Her sweater was the same brilliant blue as her eyes, which widened in surprise and pleasure the instant she recognized him.

She pushed her chair back with a clatter and sprang to her feet. The last time he'd seen her, they'd been close to the same height. Now he had a good three inches on her.

"Dustin? Omigod. It is you." She surprised him with a quick hug, sounding slightly breathless. "Wow. This is a surprise. How long has it been?"

"At least ten years." Dustin couldn't take his eyes off her. He'd never expected to see her again. "How have you been?"

"Good. I've been good." She smiled. "Congrats on the Stanley Cup MVP."

"Thanks."

"What are you doing here?"

"Meeting with Kenny." Dustin shifted his gaze to the older man, who studied him with an assessing look. "Hello, Kenny."

"Good to see you again. Thanks for coming." The older man gestured. "You two sit down now, get comfortable."

Dustin waited until Krista had resumed her seat before he pulled out a chair. The legs scraped loudly against the rough wooden floor. "If I'm interrupting—"

"You're not," Kenny insisted.

"I didn't realize you still came to Holly Pointe for the holidays," Dustin said to Krista.

"First time back in ten years. Coming was a last-minute decision." Her smile, bright and friendly, was the one he remembered. "How about you?"

"First time back for me, too. I got in last night."

"My friend and I were a day ahead of you."

Is that friend male or female? he wondered.

Not my business, he told himself, shifting his attention as Norma strode up.

"This is our best dark roast." Norma smiled as she set down

the mug. "You wanted it strong and black, and it doesn't get better than a French roast."

He lifted the cup to his lips and took a long drink. "It's great. You don't know how much I needed this."

Beaming, she set the plate with his food in front of him. "Can I get you anything else?"

"This will do it." Dustin assured her. "Thank you, Norma."

"You're very welcome." Norma shifted her focus to her husband and Krista. "Refills?"

Krista gestured to her to-go cup. "I'm still working on this, thank you."

"Me, too," Kenny told his wife.

The bells over the door jingled.

"I'll leave you to your discussion, then." Norma hurried to the counter.

Dustin took another long drink of coffee, sensing he might need the caffeine jolt. Kenny clearly had something on his mind.

Something told Dustin whatever it was also involved Krista. For the life of him, Dustin couldn't imagine what it might be.

"You two are smart, successful people," Kenny began. "Which means you no doubt suspect I'm up to something."

What Dustin thought of as Kenny's Santa Claus twinkle now danced in the older man's eyes.

Dustin took a bite of the toast and chewed, then followed up with another gulp of coffee. He waited.

"Okay, I'll bite. What are you up to, Kenny?" Krista's tone was light, but the watchful gleam in her eyes likely mirrored Dustin's own.

"I take my duty as mayor seriously." The twinkle faded, and Kenny's voice took on an urgency. "I love this town. When I ran for mayor, I vowed to do whatever I could to help our merchants thrive and keep Holly Pointe strong."

Dustin shifted uneasily in his seat, recalling the decreased foot traffic. When Kenny's gaze settled on him, he nodded to show he was listening, then took another bite.

He had questions, sure, but Dustin believed you learned far more from listening than running off at the mouth before you had all the information.

Krista wrapped long, slender fingers around her cup. Her short nails were painted a pale pink.

Dustin saw no reason to point out the lack of customers in the stores downtown. If Kenny was bringing up the topic, he was aware of that fact. What didn't make sense was why he was discussing this with two people who didn't live here, who hadn't been back in over a decade.

"Over the years, like many communities, we've experienced a drop in tourist traffic. Cabins that used to book up a year in advance often sit empty now." Worry filled Kenny's expression. "Even what we consider day traffic has been down. Those visitors who used to drive in from Maine, New Hampshire, even New York are no longer coming. Last year, we barely broke even on Holly Days, and that was with Paula's generous discount on the space."

"I'm sorry to hear that. Christmas in Holly Pointe remains one of the highlights of my childhood." Dustin downed the last of the coffee in his mug. "I don't understand why you're telling me this."

Krista shot him a glance, as if to indicate she thought he'd been too blunt when all he'd done was speak the truth. "Is there something you think we can do to help?"

The relief that washed across Kenny's weathered face told Dustin that Kenny did indeed have something in mind. If it meant giving a donation or sponsoring some activity, Dustin would be happy to pull out his wallet.

"After last season, the town council and I came up with this idea of bringing in a couple of Hollywood actors to generate publicity and draw the crowds," Kenny explained. "They were to be our *Holly*wood Stars. Get it?"

Krista smiled. "Love the play on words."

"Rosie came up with it," Kenny advised. "The woman has a knack."

Norma appeared and refilled Dustin's cup. "Unfortunately, after doing some research, we discovered even D-list actors don't come cheap."

"Since we can't afford anyone from Hollywood, we moved to plan B. We looked for local talent." Kenny chuckled. "That didn't go so well either."

Norma shook her head. "The best we could come up with was a weatherman and a retired actress who once had a bit part on a soap opera in the '80s. When even our committee members weren't impressed with those two, we tabled the project and decided to stick with traditional advertising."

"That hasn't given us the results we hoped for. So far, anyway." Kenny pulled on his beard, and his gaze grew distant. "The world is changing."

"I'm so sorry, Kenny." Krista's gaze shifted to Norma. "The world may be changing, but I believe people need what Holly Pointe has to offer."

"We agree with you. That's why we're not giving up." Kenny looked from Krista to Dustin. "Now, with international celebrities in Holly Pointe, we have hope again."

"That's good news." Dustin forked off a bite of toast and brought it to his mouth. "Who are they?"

Kenny laughed, a deep, rich ho-ho-ho. "You and Krista, of course. We want you to be our *Holly*wood Stars."

Dustin set down his fork and waited for the punch line. When none came, he kept his voice easy as he asked, "Are you serious?"

"Absolutely serious." Pushing aside his coffee cup, Kenny leaned farther forward, resting his forearms on the table. "You two are stars in your own fields. You're also part of this community. Which makes having you in this role even more special."

Two faint lines formed between Krista's brows. From the

looks of it—and her silence—she wasn't any more eager to do this than he was.

While Dustin loved this community, he'd come here to heal and stay out of the spotlight, not attract more attention. Any attention on him would bring his impending retirement to light, something he was desperate to avoid.

"Kenny, you're too kind, but I'm not a star," Krista protested. "Not the kind you need anyway."

"You're exactly who we need." Kenny shifted his gaze to Dustin. "So are you. You're local. Or as close to local as you can get without living here. You two grew up here. Every holiday we'd see you having fun with your families." Kenny glanced at his wife. "Norma would sneak you both cookies."

Dustin shot a glance at Krista, and the slight smile on her lips told him he and Ashleigh hadn't been the only ones on the receiving end of Norma's kindness.

"We've watched you grow into the fine young people you are today. We've rejoiced in your successes." Norma's voice thickened with emotion. "You're family to us."

After a long moment, Dustin heard himself ask, "What exactly would you need us to do?"

Kenny took three sheets of paper from a portfolio on the table. Keeping one for himself, he handed one to Krista and the other to Dustin. "These would be your duties."

"Selfies with the Stars in the vendor area at the barns," Krista read aloud. "Lighting of the Christmas tree. Interviews with local media outlets. Walking the red carpet at the Mistletoe Ball. Other duties as assigned." Krista looked up. "How many media interviews?"

Kenny and Norma looked at each other and shrugged. "As many as you'd want to do?"

Zero, Dustin thought grimly, that was how many interviews he wanted to do.

"What does 'other duties' mean?" Dustin asked.

"Anything you can think of that would bring people to Holly Pointe." Kenny pointed to the paper. "I'm afraid this is all we've come up with. I'm sure there's more, but, well, we're not media savvy like you two."

Dustin knew the media, all right. Reporters were exactly who he wanted to avoid until he came up with a plan. He didn't like to use the word *hiding*, but that's what he was doing in Holly Pointe. Hiding until he could come up with a plan.

The silence at the table stretched and extended. Krista offered a quick, noncommittal smile. "I'll need to check with Desz and get back to you."

"That's fine," Kenny told her, "but I need to know soon. Tomorrow morning at the latest."

Krista turned to Dustin. "Desz is the friend I mentioned before. She came with me from New York to enjoy the holidays. I need to take her feelings about the time commitment on this into account."

Dustin nodded, then looked at Kenny. "What's your backup plan? What will you do if we can't help?"

"You are my backup plan." Kenny's normally jovial expression turned grim. "This is our last shot to help the town. If you and Krista can't do it, this will likely be the last Holly Days we'll have."

Krista's shocked gaze shifted to Norma.

Norma answered her unspoken question with a nod.

"What do you say?" Kenny leaned forward, his gaze sliding from Krista to Dustin. "Will you two be our *Holly*wood Stars?"

CHAPTER FOUR

Dustin fell into step beside Krista as she started back toward the cabin. "Mind if I walk with you?"

She offered him a quick smile. "I'd like that."

When she'd seen him at the Busy Bean, Krista had been unprepared for the punch. The last time she'd seen Dustin Bellamy, he'd been a boy. There was a world of difference between the boy she'd crushed on and the man strolling beside her.

The adult Dustin was taller, his shoulders broader and his body more muscular. His hair was now more of a sandy blond, and his gorgeous, smoky gray eyes, instead of sparkling with devilment like they used to, were watchful.

Dustin's square jaw and classically handsome features would always draw the eye, but the slight bump on his nose from a break kept him from being too pretty.

"Where are you staying?" she asked conversationally.

"I rented the same cabin my family used to rent."

The Jeep. "I'm right next door."

"No kidding?"

The quicksilver smile that had his eyes crinkling at the

corners had her saying to herself, *Yes, there he is. That's the Dustin I remember.*

"The thought of no more Holly Days makes me feel sick."

He only nodded.

She slanted a glance at him. "I wish I could believe Kenny was exaggerating, but the lack of people on the street, even my cabin being available at the last minute, appears to support that he's right to worry."

One beat of silence, then two.

"It sounds as if you're seriously considering taking on the role of *Holly*wood Star?"

Krista chuckled at the term, then sobered. "I want to help. If Desz is okay with it, then yes, I'll do it. What about you?"

He shook his head. "It's a hard pass for me."

Krista didn't bother to hide her surprise. "Why so definitive?"

"I came here specifically for some R&R, to get away from everything." A muscle in Dustin's jaw jumped. "Not to be plunged back into the limelight."

Something more was going on here, Krista thought, but she didn't push. "I understand, I really do. When you're in the spot-light, you often need to fully step out of it in order to relax and recharge."

The tight set to his jaw eased, and she realized he'd expected her to argue. That wasn't happening. Unless he'd changed, she knew Dustin Bellamy couldn't be pushed into anything.

"What brought you here?" Dustin asked.

"Last-minute impulse." She gave a careless shrug. "I thought I'd be working, but ended up having time off."

"It's crazy being neighbors again after all these years." Now that the *Holly*wood Star issue was seemingly off the table, his smile came easily.

Krista chuckled. "My parents are never going to believe it."

"How are they?"

"They're good. My brother and his wife just had their first baby. Mom and Dad are spending Christmas with them."

His eyes widened. "Little Tommy has a wife and a baby?"

"Little Tommy is six-two, and it's Tom now." Krista tried for a serious tone, but ruined the effect with a smile. "A tax attorney named Tommy just doesn't have the same panache."

Dustin chuckled. "You're right about that."

They fell into a familiar rhythm as they walked the winding bike trail leading to the cabins.

"What about your family?" she asked.

"My parents will be with Ashleigh and the grandkids this year. Four boys under the age of eight."

"Wow. Four." Krista barely remembered Dustin's sister. She'd been at least six or seven years older than her, so to Krista, she'd seemed more like another adult than a peer.

"When Ash starts talking about preschools and playdates, I feel my eyes glaze over."

Krista laughed. "It's like that for me when Tom talks about pulling an all-nighter…with the baby."

"Speaking of all-nighters," Dustin shoved his hands into his coat pockets as the wind picked up, "remember our night of ice fishing?"

"I can't believe I let you talk me into that." Krista chuckled as she shook her head. "When you promised a hut and a fire, I never thought it'd still be so cold. And to be clear, we didn't pull an all-nighter. I may have had to sneak in, but I was home by two."

"It was fun." Dustin's smile flashed. "If you remember, I did my best to keep you warm."

"I remember." Even now, Krista's body heated as she remembered the kisses they'd shared in the ice hut that night. "I wish we'd caught at least one fish. Still, when the topic of ice fishing comes up, at least I can say I tried it."

Dustin blinked. "Has it come up?"

"Not yet, but if it does, I'm prepared."

He grinned, and she smiled back, basking in the resurgence of their connection.

Dustin paused by the Jeep and gestured to the cabin. "Home sweet home."

Despite the light tone, he sounded as disappointed as Krista felt.

"This might sound strange, but when I walked into my family's old cabin again, it felt as if I was coming home." Krista massaged her brow, where a headache threatened to form. "I don't want Holly Days to go under, Dustin. I want other families to have the opportunity we had to build memories here."

His expression remained somber as his gray eyes searched hers.

"I'm going to help Kenny." She blew out a breath. "I'll square it with Desz, but I'll find a way to make it work."

"I'm sure he'll be grateful. Kenny certainly couldn't have a better star than you." Dustin turned, then paused at the base of the porch steps to look over his shoulder. "It was good seeing you again."

Disappointment squeezed Krista's heart as she entered her cabin. While she'd meant what she told Dustin about understanding his need for R&R, she'd secretly hoped his love for Holly Pointe would override that need.

"I want to say I approve," Desz called out in greeting and stepped back from the window.

Puzzled, Krista frowned. "Approve of what?"

"Mystery man." Desz's dark eyes twinkled. "I assume that was Kenny's surprise. Santa found Mr. Perfect and wanted to give you an early Christmas gift."

Krista lifted her hands. "Still clueless."

"The golden-haired Adonis occupying the cabin next door. He

looks familiar, but I can't quite place him." Desz pretended to fan her face. "Man, that guy is built. When you add a gorgeous face to the mix, well, pardon me while I stick my face in a bowl of cold water to cool off."

How was it, Krista thought, *that Desz could always make her smile?* "That hunk is Dustin Bellamy."

Recognition flashed in Desz's dark eyes. "Stanley Cup MVP Dustin Bellamy?"

After removing her coat and hanging it on the vintage coat tree near the door, Krista dropped into a chair. "I didn't realize you followed hockey."

"Not for the hockey, but for the gorgeous." Desz's gaze searched hers as she took a seat on the sofa. "You look flustered. Do I need to get two bowls of cold water?"

Krista shook her head and, raking a hand through her hair, blew out a breath. "It's what he didn't say that has me all hot and bothered."

"Clear as mud. Continue."

That prompted another smile. "Dustin and his family used to come to Holly Point every year. They stayed in the same cabin he's in now."

"Right next to yours."

"Yes. We used to joke we were next-door neighbors for two weeks every year." Krista resisted the urge to sigh. "Anyway, Kenny heard Dustin was in town and asked him to come to the Busy Bean to meet with him."

"Before or after your meeting?"

"Same time." When Desz's lips started to curve upward, Krista held up a hand. "Not to hook us up, but to make us an offer. He asked Dustin and me to be Holly Days' *Holly*wood Stars."

"Now it's your turn to explain."

"*Holly*wood, emphasis on Holly because of Holly Days. Get it?"

"Love it." Desz's eyes snapped with excitement. "When do your *Holly*wood duties begin?"

"No start date yet." Krista shook her head. "I can't believe that after having just lost a major international campaign, *this* is my new assignment."

"I think it sounds intriguing. What does it involve?"

Taking a breath, Krista laid out the conversation with Kenny. Knowing Desz's love of details, Krista made sure not to leave anything out, including the fact that she and Dustin had yet to give Kenny a final answer.

"You're going to do it, of course."

"I wanted to speak with you before giving Kenny an answer." Krista hesitated. "I want you to be honest with me, Desz. We came to enjoy the holiday together, not for me to—"

"Hey, big girl here. I'll have no trouble keeping myself occupied." Desz waved a dismissive hand. "Being in Holly Pointe is like gazing into an open candy chest. I can't wait to start digging through the contents."

"Love the imagery, Desz. You should be a writer."

Though a smile tugged at the corners of her lips, Desz somehow managed to keep her expression serious. "Hey, maybe I'll start a blog."

"Great idea," Krista exclaimed, then returned to the topic at hand. "I don't believe this *Holly*wood Stars thing will take all that much time…"

"No matter how much time it takes, do it." Desz met Krista's gaze, suddenly serious. "It's not often you get a chance to play a starring role in saving a community's holiday traditions."

"That's why I was willing to at least consider doing what I could to make it work." Krista pressed her lips together. "I don't see why everyone can't see the importance."

Desz's brow arched. "Everyone?"

"Dustin won't do it."

"Why?"

Krista thought back to their conversation. "He said he came here for R&R, not to work."

"That's understandable."

"I know. It's just that…" Krista's voice rang with disappointment edged with irritation. "I thought he loved Holly Days as much as I do."

"Maybe he's still recovering from that injury he sustained in the finals last summer."

"He walks okay." Krista pulled her brows together in thought. "I didn't notice him limping or anything. Something else is going on. I just wish I knew what it was."

Desz leaned back against the sofa, her gaze turning speculative. "How well did you know him back then?"

"We spent time together." Krista waved an airy hand. "I mean, he *was* right next door."

Desz's gaze sharpened. "I sense more than simple friendship between you two. Am I wrong?"

Sometimes, Desz could be a little too perceptive.

"I guess you could say Dustin Bellamy was my holiday heart-throb." Krista tried to keep her tone light, but emotion crept into her voice. "For two weeks every year, I was basically in love with the boy next door. Then I'd go back to Ohio, he'd return to Minnesota, and we wouldn't see each other again until the next year."

Desz brought a hand to her chest and thumped it against her heart. "It's like that old movie. Oh, what was it called?"

With Desz's expectant gaze fixed on her, Krista felt compelled to answer. "*Same Time, Next Year?*"

"That's the one." Desz pointed. "It's just like—"

"It's not at all like that movie." Krista laughed. "That couple was married and cheating on their spouses."

"Okay, not exactly the same. The point is they cared for each other and built a solid relationship despite only seeing each other once a year." Desz brought one finger to her bright red lips as her gaze grew thoughtful. "Did Dustin return your feelings?"

"We were kids, Desz," Krista protested.

"The last time you were here, you were seventeen," Desz pointed out.

When Krista hesitated, Desz continued. "You just told me he was your holiday heartthrob and admitted to being in love with him for two weeks every year. I'm simply wondering if those feelings went both ways."

"I thought they did. We had so much fun together. Back then, Holly Days was mostly outdoor stuff." As she thought back, Krista's lips curved, and her heart became a sweet mass in her chest. "We did everything together. The tree lighting, the Christmas singalong, even pond hockey. He played. I cheered him and the other players on."

Desz circled one hand in the air. "Did you and he ever…?"

"We did our share of kissing. That's as far as it went." Krista's lips curved. "I really liked him, Desz. He was…nice. Smart, athletic and nice."

"How did things end?"

"The last time I saw him, he and his family left unexpectedly on Christmas Eve day. Apparently, they'd gotten a call from a neighbor who'd been watching their house. A pipe had broken and flooded the downstairs." Krista shook her head. "They didn't even stay for the Mistletoe Ball that evening."

"The climax to the Holly Days festivities," Desz murmured, recounting what Krista had told her on the drive to Holly Pointe.

"I'd looked forward to the ball all year. You had to be at least a senior in high school to attend." Even now, Krista could see the shimmery gown she'd planned to wear. "I had this amazing red dress. It would have been my first time dancing with Dustin." Krista shrugged. "Not meant to be."

"Not to worry." Desz's lips curved up in a sly smile. "I promise. I'm going to get you that long-overdue dance."

It wasn't until Krista went inside her cabin that Dustin realized he'd forgotten about the food market. This time, instead of walking, he hopped into the Jeep.

He returned with enough staples to feed an army. Once everything was put away, he did his exercises. Despite what the doctor had said, Dustin wouldn't let his training slide. The rest of the day passed swiftly. He thought about going to the Barns at Grace Hollow that evening to check out the Marketplace, but decided to stay home.

Last night had been a late one, and he'd been up early to meet with Kenny.

Thinking of Kenny had Dustin picking up his phone. He really should text the mayor and let him know he wasn't interested in being a *Holly*wood Star.

He hesitated, recalling the disappointed look in Krista's eyes when he'd told her it was a hard pass for him. He set down the phone. Tomorrow morning would be soon enough, he decided, crossing the room to the window facing Krista's cabin.

Though the cabins were identical in size and style, the interior floor plans were flip-flopped. Lights inside the cabin next door cast a golden glow through the windows and onto the snowy landscape.

Smoke curled from the chimney. It was crazy to think that, after all these years, Krista was right next door.

Dustin had missed her with an intensity that shocked him after his family had quit coming to Holly Pointe. Hockey might have been his life during the rest of the year, but those two weeks in Holly Pointe had been his off-season, his time to relax and have fun.

He and Krista had been only twelve the year they started spending time together. She'd been his buddy, a blast to be around with a quick mind and a sense of humor that never turned mean. If anything went wrong, she'd always been there to lighten the mood. Even after all these years, he considered her to be the sweetest girl he'd ever known.

Dustin let the curtain drop and stepped back as memories flooded him. He remembered her cheering for both teams at the pond hockey games, because the thought of anyone losing made her sad.

When he'd first confided his dream of playing for the NHL, she hadn't laughed. Instead, her expression had turned fierce as she told him he'd make it happen.

That last Christmas, she'd been so excited about the gift she'd gotten him that she'd insisted on giving it to him early. The mug, bearing two crossed hockey sticks and the words "Future NHL Superstar," had been something he'd treasured. He'd kept it for years, until a careless roommate had broken it.

Dustin strode to the table where he'd tossed the sheet Kenny had given him and picked it up. He let his gaze linger on the listed duties before dropping the paper.

Krista was good to everyone, so it didn't surprise him that she'd want to help Kenny.

When he finally climbed the stairs to his bedroom on the second level—the one on the main floor might be bigger, but in his mind it would always be his parents' room—Dustin found himself stepping to the window.

How many times in the past had he stood there, waiting for Krista to appear so they could wave good night? Too many times to count, he realized.

Dustin wasn't sure how long he stood at the window. Then, as if this were a dream, the light flicked on, and Krista appeared.

If she was startled to see him, it didn't show. Smiling, she lifted a hand and gave a little wave.

Dustin found himself smiling back as he did the same.

Then, as she had in years past, she pulled down the shades and left him standing there, thinking of her.

CHAPTER FIVE

Krista, with an eager Desz beside her, arrived early the next day for her first duty as a *Holly*wood Star. On tap for today was Selfies with the Stars. Or rather, with a single star, as it would be just her.

She'd hoped, really hoped, Dustin would have a change of heart. But she'd heard nothing from him since he'd walked her home, though they had shared their good-night wave, a blast from the past that still made her smile.

"Wow." Krista paused at the walkway leading to the Barns at Grace Hollow. The pictures she'd seen hadn't done the structures justice. Nestled between tall pines, the two equally impressive barns constructed of reclaimed lumber, stone and steel stole her breath.

"Double wow," Desz agreed, following Krista to the smaller barn first.

Krista glanced in the window. "Love all the stained glass. This one appears to be some sort of chapel."

"I bet they use it for weddings, small receptions, stuff like that." Desz remained at the window a few seconds more before stepping back. "I can't wait to see inside the big one."

The "big one" rose nearly three stories and was decorated for the holidays with white lights and greenery. Signs outside the building announced that the "Holly Days' Marketplace" ran from ten to seven p.m. every day until December 23.

Desz nudged Krista's arm. "Those are fabulous pics."

Krista shifted her gaze. An enormous poster boasted giant images of her and Dustin.

"Oh no." Krista's heart lurched. "There are going to be a lot of disappointed fans this evening. Dustin must not have told Kenny he wouldn't be here."

"Who isn't here?"

Krista whirled.

Dressed in chinos and a sweater, Dustin grinned at her.

"What are you doing here?" Krista asked, wondering why she sounded irritated when she was so glad to see him.

If he noticed the edge to her voice, it didn't show.

"A guy can only handle so much R&R." He lifted his broad hands. "I gave Kenny's proposal more thought. No reason I can't toss a little work into the mix. Especially for a good cause."

Though she'd sensed there was more to his initial hesitation than simply an aversion to working while on a holiday, her faith —her once-unshakable faith—in him was restored.

Krista found herself oh-so-tempted to fling her arms around him and give him a hug. Instead, she settled for grinning back. "You're going to do it."

He nodded as his smoky eyes remained fixed on her. "I told Kenny this morning."

Everything around them faded. In that moment, it was just her and Dustin as the connection pulsed and tightened between them.

She moved closer to him.

He moved closer to her.

Only a foot separated them when Desz, whom Krista had

forgotten all about, spoke. "Hi. I'm Desz Presley. It's good to meet you."

Dustin quickly rallied, offering Desz a heart-stopping smile. "You're the friend who came with Krista to Holly Pointe. It's good to meet you."

Krista's phone buzzed a warning. She glanced at Dustin. "We have ten minutes to get onstage."

"I'm exploring." Desz wiggled her fingers. "Smile big. Well, not too big. You don't want to look like clowns."

Krista laughed as Desz slipped into the crowd.

Conscious of Dustin's palm resting lightly at the small of her back, Krista quickly reached the raised platform that displayed a winter forest background, complete with pine trees that glittered.

Letters at the top of the scene spelled out Holly Days and the year. Krista had to give it to Kenny, or whoever was in charge of this activity. Each time someone posted their selfie online, Holly Days would be promoted.

A blonde woman, who'd been issuing instructions to two men about keeping the line moving, flashed a smile when Krista and Dustin approached.

"You're here." Relief blanketed the young woman's face. "I'm Lucy Cummings, Paula Franks's daughter. I'll be assisting you today."

Ah, yes, Krista thought, recognizing the name. Paula Franks was the woman who owned the barns. She'd also given Kenny a great price on the space.

"This is Kevin Johnson." Lucy gestured to the blond man and then the brown-haired one. "And his brother, Sam. "They're here to keep the fans in line."

"Thanks for agreeing to do this." Kevin's smile came easy and fast.

"Holly Days is special to all of us," Sam added.

Dustin gestured with one hand toward a line that already

stretched out of sight. "You want to bet 95% of these people are here to get a selfie with Krista?"

Kevin laughed. "I think there may be one or two for you. We've got a lot of hockey fans in this area."

Krista glanced at Lucy, who was now focused on making adjustments to an impressive camera. "I thought these were selfies."

"That's the plan, but if someone doesn't have a phone or a camera with them, I'll take a picture and email it to them for five dollars." Lucy smiled. "I'm not a professional, but I know my way around a camera."

"You take fabulous photographs." Kevin brushed his lips carelessly across her mass of blonde hair.

When Lucy turned to him, the love in his eyes had Krista fighting a twinge of envy. Krista had done her share of dating, but had never taken the time to focus on a relationship.

When Kevin put his arms around Lucy's waist and pulled her close for a kiss, Krista shifted her gaze to Dustin.

"I haven't had a chance to say it yet, but you look amazing," Dustin told her.

"I decided to go with casual, rather than high fashion." Krista swept a hand down as if modeling her red cashmere tunic, leggings and black heeled boots.

"Excellent choice." Dustin smiled. "I like the twisty thing you did with your hair."

The admiration in his eyes had Krista going warm all over.

"Did you sleep well last night?" he asked, his tone low.

His question jolted her back to the shock of seeing him at the window last night. When she'd spotted him standing there, their years apart had simply fallen away. She'd loved their nightly ritual and recalled telling him on more than one occasion that she always slept better afterward. "I did. How about you?"

"Krista. Dustin." Lucy's voice broke through her déjà vu fog. "Your fans await."

Krista glanced to the line growing longer by the second.

"I'm seeing a lot of hockey sticks." Krista offered Dustin a wink. "It's a wild guess, but I'm betting those fans are here for you."

～

After only fifteen minutes, Dustin concluded that posing for selfies with fans was more pleasure than work.

"Would you mind signing this for my grandson?" An older man held out a hockey stick and a Sharpie.

Out of the corner of his eye, Dustin saw Krista gently maneuvering a young girl so she faced the camera at a more flattering angle.

"I'd be happy to sign it," Dustin told the man.

"My grandson's name is Jax. J-A-X," the man said. "He's a hockey fanatic."

Dustin paused for a second, then wrote, *Jax, Keep the fire in your heart. Dustin Bellamy.*

The older man's brown eyes filled with tears. "He's going to love this. His dad, my son, he died this year in an accident. It's been hard on all of us."

"I'm sorry." Dustin handed the stick back to the man. "Would you like a picture?"

The man shook his head. "My wife has the phone."

"Let me take one, and I'll email it to you," Lucy offered. "You and Dustin get together and hold up the stick."

Dustin noticed Lucy didn't say anything about the five-dollar fee.

To his left, Dustin heard Krista telling a young girl that she was originally from Ohio, too.

Dustin lost track of time. Though he'd dreaded today, he enjoyed talking hockey to fans who loved the game as much as he did.

There was only one tough moment. A teenage boy had brought a team jersey bearing Dustin's No. 44 for him to sign. Once he did, the boy held it up for the selfie.

It struck Dustin that he'd never again wear No. 44 or be part of that team. The guys who wore the same jerseys were no longer his teammates. The pain he fought so hard to keep under wraps surged.

He started when Krista's hand settled on his arm. "Time's up, hotshot."

Dustin expelled a breath and realized he'd been staring into space. Seeing the concern in her eyes, he smiled and forced a light tone. "That went fast."

"It did. I had fun." Her blue eyes studied him. "How was it for you?"

"I enjoyed it." He had, even though the event had hammered home his current situation. That had him realizing the last thing he wanted to do tonight was sit in his cabin alone and brood. "Do you have plans for the evening?"

She inclined her head. "What do you have in mind?"

"Dinner? Or something else? Anything else." Once again, the Player with the Plan didn't have one. "Whatever you want."

Well, that was smooth, he thought with disgust.

"I wouldn't want to leave Desz out—" Krista's phone dinged. She lifted a finger. "Give me a sec."

Pulling the small phone from her pocket, she read the text, then replied before smiling up at Dustin. "As it turns out, Desz met a potter she wants to interview, and they're having dinner together. She invited me to join them, but I'd rather spend the evening with you."

"Great." Conscious they still stood onstage, Dustin took her arm. "Let's find somewhere more private where we can decide our next step."

~

Krista told herself she was being ridiculous. Dustin barely touched her, and all of a sudden, her heart was tripping all over itself.

She'd spent the past ten years surrounded by handsome, accomplished men. There had been a few who'd garnered a second look, but none had been capable of throwing her off-balance with one touch.

Trying to ignore the heat seeping through her sweater where his fingers lingered, she stepped with him to the edge of the stage where Kevin stood.

"Watch your step," Kevin warned as they navigated the metal steps. Once they reached the bottom, he handed them each a bottle of water. "I thought you might be thirsty after all that smiling and talking."

"Kevin." Lucy's voice rang out.

The man's gaze shifted to where the blonde stood with several vendors. He flashed a smile. "Duty calls."

Krista watched him go. She liked Lucy's boyfriend. Liked that he was friendly without being flirty. One of her hot buttons was men who flirted when they had a girlfriend.

Dustin flipped open the cap of his water and downed half the bottle in one gulp.

"You were thirsty." Krista brought her own bottle to her lips.

His gaze slid to her and settled on her mouth. She took a sip, then lowered the bottle, her lips tingling.

"I didn't realize I was," Dustin admitted, "but Kevin was right. Talking and smiling is hard work."

"Don't give me that," she teased. "I was right beside you. You're a natural."

Krista had discovered during the last hour that not only was Dustin easy on the eyes, he possessed a genuine warmth and a true passion for hockey that came through loud and clear.

She'd heard him hesitate only when asked when he'd be returning to the team.

Krista didn't follow hockey, though she had enjoyed the pond hockey games when she'd been in Holly Pointe. And she had watched Dustin play in the Stanley Cup Finals earlier this year, unable to believe that formidable competitor had once been her holiday heartthrob.

Dustin finished off the water. For a second, his gaze turned distant. Then he blinked, and the clouds disappeared. He gestured with the hand holding the empty bottle. "I expected people to leave once they got their selfies, but it appears most of them stayed to shop."

"I noticed the same thing." From her position behind the ropes, Krista gazed out over the crowded floor. "Selfies with the Stars brought them in, and the amazing Marketplace offerings enticed them to stay."

Absently, Krista took a sip of water. "I'm wondering if what Kenny has us doing is enough."

"Do you seriously want to add to our duties?"

Krista relaxed when she saw the teasing glint in Dustin's eyes. "We could do more. I know we could. Desz is interviewing a potter right now for her blog. What if we interviewed one of the shopkeepers in town? Or an artisan here in the Marketplace? We could video it and put the interview up on the town's website. Would you be up for that?"

"Would we do these interviews together or separately?"

"Either would work."

He smiled. "If it's together, I'm in."

Krista impulsively looped her arm through his. "Together it is."

"Sorry I had to rush off."

Krista and Dustin turned as one toward the sound of Kevin's voice.

"Everything okay?" Krista asked.

Kevin waved a dismissive hand. "Problem with an electrical cord. All handled."

"This place seems to be a well-run operation," Dustin commented.

"All because of Lucy." Kevin gave all the credit to his girl-friend. "The numbers of people who showed up for your Selfies with the Stars event..." Kevin put his fingers together, then exploded them. "Blew us out of the water."

"Kevin's right." Sam appeared and nodded his agreement. "Couldn't have gone any better. Ah, since we're closing up, Lucy asked me to show you to the side exit so you can avoid most of the crowd."

"Appreciate it." Dustin glanced around. "Where is Lucy?"

"Handling the next crisis." Kevin chuckled. "Before my brother takes you away, if you're free tomorrow afternoon, I'd love for you to come out and see my horses, take a ride."

"They're Icelandic," Sam informed them. "I guarantee you haven't seen any horses like these."

Dustin nodded. "Give me the time and place, and I'll be there."

Kevin shifted his attention to Krista. "What about you?"

Regret blanketed Krista's face. "I came to Holly Pointe with a friend. I don't want to leave her on her own—"

"Bring her along." Kevin smiled. "The more the merrier."

Still, Krista hesitated. "I'm not sure if Desz has ever ridden a horse. I have, but it's been a long time."

Kevin waved aside her worries. "These horses are gentle. No previous riding experience necessary."

"In that case," Krista smiled, "I accept."

Dustin touched her arm. "The three of us can drive there together. I know the way."

Surprise flickered in Kevin's eyes. "You do?"

"I ran into Derek Kelly earlier today. He mentioned your family bought the old Riverton place. Like my dad, Mr. Riverton was big into model trains." Dustin remembered how his father had made an effort every year to see the elderly widower. "My dad and I went out there at least once every time we were in Holly Pointe."

Krista smiled. "I didn't go *every* year with Dustin and his Dad, but I went at least two times. Mr. Riverton showed us something he called a Halloween General set. Do you remember that one, Dustin?"

Dustin pulled his brows together. "Vaguely."

"It had an orange and black locomotive, and the passenger car was blue."

"How do you remember that?" Dustin asked, amazed.

Krista shrugged. "Blue was my favorite color back then, and I thought the locomotive was spooky cool."

Sam and Kevin exchanged glances.

"I didn't realize the two of you were so well acquainted." Kevin's eyes held a curious glint.

Dustin grinned. "Krista and I, we go way back."

The lights overhead flickered on and off.

Krista glanced up at the ceiling. "Another electrical issue?"

"Not at all." With a clipboard in hand, Lucy hurried to them. "Just reminding people that the Marketplace is closing for the day," Lucy answered as she strolled up. "I'm surprised you two aren't out the door by now."

"We're heading there." Dustin paused. "Hey, do you have suggestions on something that'd be fun for Krista and I to do this evening?"

"Dobson's Hill," Lucy and Kevin said in unison.

A light flared in Dustin's eyes. His gaze slid to Krista. "The hill close to Landers Tree Farm."

"I remember." Krista lifted her hands, then let them drop. "Unfortunately, no sled."

"I have a couple in the bed of my truck you can use." Lucy

smiled. "Kevin, Sam and I were out there just this morning. The snow is perfect for sledding."

Krista brought the hill into focus in her head. "Are there lights out there now?"

"Yep, put in two, or maybe three, years back," Kevin advised.

"I can't wait to see them." Krista made a sweeping gesture with one hand to include Kevin and Sam. "Thanks again for everything you did to make this event a success."

"Well, Kevin is crazy about Christmas, and Sam is one of Holly Pointe's best cheerleaders, so they're always up for helping." Lucy's blue eyes softened. "We loved having you here today."

"You made it painless," Dustin said, agreeing with Krista. "Thanks."

After another minute of conversation, Krista and Dustin followed Sam down a long hallway.

"I'll meet you at Lucy's truck," Sam told Dustin.

Dustin nodded.

"I'm going to meet Sam at the back of the building, where Lucy's truck is parked, and grab the sleds." Dustin's gaze turned questioning. "How about once we get to the cabins and change, we drive out to Dobson's Hill together?"

"Can I ask one favor first?"

"Anything." He stepped close. "What do you need?"

Krista found herself once again aware of just how big, how strong and how utterly male he was.

"A ride home." Krista gave a little laugh. "Desz took the car."

CHAPTER SIX

Once back at the cabin, Krista grabbed something quick to eat, then changed into her cold-weather gear. She shot Desz a swift text.

Going sledding with Dustin. Interested?

The response came quickly. *Still at Rosie's. Have fun.*

As Krista walked to the cabin next door, she found herself smiling. She couldn't recall the last time she'd taken time for fun in the snow.

She gave three sharp raps on Dustin's door.

He opened it immediately.

"Come in." He motioned her inside. "I just need to get on my boots."

Stepping inside, Krista pulled the door shut behind her. One quick glance told her this cabin could benefit from some updating. The rug on the hardwood floor had thinned in several spots, and a stuffed moose head, complete with antlers, still hung over the fireplace.

"That is…" She tried not to wince. "Incredibly tacky."

Dustin, who'd dropped down on the sofa to pull boots on over thick, woolen socks, grinned.

"Every year, my dad went on and on about how much he loved that moose." Dustin chuckled. "Saying it always got my mom going."

"I love your dad, but I'm siding with your mother on this one."

"You and she always did get along."

"I liked her. So did my mom."

After lacing his boots, Dustin stood. "Ready for an adventure in the great outdoors?"

She gestured to the ski pants and jacket. "I certainly didn't dress like this for a night on the town."

As Krista slid into the Jeep, anticipation surged. She thought of the night ahead, sledding under a sky filled with stars while in the company of an intelligent and fascinating man.

Who needed a night on the town?

The instant Krista stepped from his Jeep and into the brisk north wind, Dustin watched her pull her neck gaiter over her nose. With the hood covering her dark hair, the only thing visible were her gorgeous blue eyes that sparkled with excitement.

Dustin realized in her current garb she was likely unrecognizable to the twenty or so sledders on Dobson's Hill. He supposed no one would recognize him either. That was just the way he wanted it.

He'd spent enough time today socializing and talking hockey. Tonight, he wanted to simply relax and enjoy his time with Krista.

"The hill seems steeper than I remember." Krista's comment broke through his thoughts.

Dustin studied the snow-covered mound and nodded. "The lights are a good addition. Otherwise, even with a full moon, it'd be too dark to sled."

"I can't wait."

Letting her excitement infuse him, Dustin pulled the sleds out of the back of the Jeep. Two saucers and one toboggan.

"I'll carry these." Krista lifted the plastic saucers from his hands.

"It's no trouble," he protested, but she only shook her head.

Dustin could easily carry all three up the hill. He might be on injured reserve, but he worked out every day. He liked keeping in shape, and the exercises and weights were part of his daily routine. He found comfort in the familiar.

"I like doing my part." Krista wrapped her arms around the saucers and hugged them close to her chest.

"You always did," Dustin murmured.

"I'll take that as a compliment."

"Good, because it was meant as one." He remembered her as a good sport and someone determined to pull her own weight.

As Dustin stared into eyes filled with intelligence and humor, the years simply melted away.

Was it any wonder she'd been his best friend in Holly Pointe? Or that he'd missed her like crazy every time his family had returned to Minnesota? He'd briefly considered trying to stay in touch, but even at seventeen he'd been realistic enough to know a long-distance romance wouldn't work.

He'd had big plans for the future. As had she.

But, oh, how he'd missed her. And he was happy, thrilled really, to be with her again.

Their eyes remained locked until, tipping her head back, Krista shifted to study the hill and the path that others had worn through the snow to the crest.

Without warning, she took off, calling over her shoulder, "Meet you at the top."

∼

By the time she reached the crest of the hill, Krista was out of breath. She tried to tell herself it was because she'd hurried to match Dustin's long strides when he'd caught up with her. But she knew the real reason.

Him.

Her heart galloped as she thought of the electricity that had crackled between them at the base of the hill. An electricity that had her wanting to kiss him.

Dustin shot her a wicked grin as he set down the massive toboggan that was long enough for four adults. He gestured to it with one hand. "Care for a spin?"

Krista dumped the saucers by a tree. "I thought you'd never ask."

She underestimated the intimacy of a ride down the hill with him. With Dustin's muscular thighs encasing her and his arms around her to steer, she didn't worry about the cold wind or plunging temperatures. Heat, strong and pulsing, flowed through her veins.

Did he feel it, too?

After the third—or was it the fourth?—trip down the hill on the toboggan, they switched to the saucers.

Krista screamed each time she sailed down the steep hill, careening over little bumps and dips, her bright blue saucer spinning her around once she reached the bottom.

Dustin appeared to be trying to see how long he could keep his red saucer airborne.

After their third trip down, he took her arm as they climbed the hill together.

"I've had a blast," Krista told him. "But this will be my last trip down. I have snow in one of my boots, and my hands are freezing."

"We don't have to go down again," he told her. "Let's grab the toboggan and call it a night."

Krista paused. "You don't mind?"

He winked. "There's snow in my boots, too."

Once they were back in the Jeep with the heat blasting, Dustin slanted a glance in her direction. "It's still early."

Krista's heart somersaulted, but her voice came out steady and offhand. "What do you have in mind?"

"Beer and a movie?"

Krista thought of Desz and felt a stab of guilt. "I'm not sure if Desz is home yet, but if she is, I—"

"Ask her to join us," Dustin immediately offered. "It'll give her and me a chance to get better acquainted."

Deep in her heart, Krista knew Dustin would rather the two of them be alone together. The offer spoke to his generosity of spirit. "I'll text her."

Krista's fingers flew across the keyboard on her phone screen. Coverage could be spotty in this area, or it had been way back when.

Interested in a movie night with Dustin and me?

The answer came back in a matter of seconds.

Working on blog. Can you watch at his place?

Sure, Krista texted back.

A thumbs-up was Desz's response.

"What's the verdict?" Dustin asked.

"She's busy writing." Krista tried not to smile. "Is it okay if we watch the movie at your place? That way, we won't disturb her."

"Sounds like a plan." Dustin turned onto the highway leading back into Holly Pointe and his shoulders relaxed against the seat. A comfortable silence filled the interior of the Jeep.

Dustin slanted a quick glance in her direction before refocusing on the snow-covered road. "I spoke with my parents earlier today. They said to tell you hello."

He continued before Krista could respond. "It was a chaotic call. Ashleigh's two older boys were in the background and wouldn't stop talking. My dad finally put them on the phone." Dustin's lips curved. "They're great kids."

"I can't wait until my niece is old enough to talk."

"Mason, that's Ashleigh's oldest, turns eight in February."

"That's crazy."

"Sometimes," Dustin said slowly, "it feels that while I was pursuing my dream, life went on and left me behind. I sometimes wonder if everything I gave up was worth it."

Another woman might have offered platitudes. Krista understood the second-guessing and the doubts that surfaced at night in the quiet.

"It's only natural to wonder." Reaching over, Krista placed her palm against his arm and let it linger there for several seconds. "For me, all the sacrifice was worth it. I'd hazard to say it was worth it to you as well. We pursued our passion and were successful. Now, we're…or rather, *I'm* poised to begin anew."

The questioning glance he slanted at her reminded her he didn't know the seriousness of her current situation.

"I lost out on a big account earlier this month. A couple years ago, they'd have picked me. This time, they chose a nineteen-year-old."

"I knew you at seventeen," he reminded her. "I'd say you look exactly the same, but you're actually even more beautiful now."

Krista shook her head. "What a line."

Dustin brought his hand to his heart. "No line. A simple statement of fact."

"Thanks for that." Her lips quirked up in a rueful smile. "Unfortunately, most advertisers want young and fresh."

"One has to be realistic," he said, almost to himself.

Krista expelled a breath. "Yes, I have to face facts."

"I never considered you might be facing your own Waterloo." He spoke so softly that for a second Krista wondered if she'd imagined the words. Then he continued. "Hockey is a demanding sport. You've probably heard I was injured in the finals but continued to play."

"The sportscasters were in awe of your performance." Krista

saw no reason to mention the speculation about the extent of his injury and whether he'd ever play again.

"I gave those last games everything I had." Dustin's tone held no emotion. "Though I'd do it again, the decision to play while injured came at a price."

Krista chose her words carefully. "Your ACL still bothers you?"

"Despite all the rehab I've done in the months since, I'm not back to a hundred percent." Dustin pulled the Jeep to a stop in front of his cabin. "Let's get inside. You need to get the snow out of your boot and warm up."

What did it say that warming up brought a far different image to mind than he'd likely intended with the casual comment?

Once inside, Dustin stoked the fire as Krista sat on the sofa and removed her boots. She'd misspoken. She had snow in *both* boots.

The second boot had barely hit the floor when Dustin appeared with a towel and a pair of wool socks.

"Thanks." Once the dry socks were on, Krista moved to the fireplace, holding out her hands to bask in the warmth radiating from the hearth.

"I know I mentioned beer, but would you rather have something hot?" he asked.

"Something hot sounds heavenly."

"What would you like?"

She inclined her head. "What are my choices?"

"Hot cocoa from a mix. Coffee." His brow furrowed in thought. "There's also a tin of some kind of herbal tea in the cupboard that I saw when I got here. I think I'll give that a try."

"I'd love some herbal tea, too." She turned away from the fire. "Why don't I make us both a cup? While I do, you can take off your boots and get on some dry socks."

When he hesitated, she smiled. "You don't want me to be the only one with warm feet, do you?"

Shaking his head, he laughed. "I guess not."

Ten minutes later, the tea was ready, their feet were both encased in wool socks, and Dustin had positioned the sofa so it faced the crackling fire.

Dustin took a sip of tea. "This isn't half bad."

"I love the taste." Krista smiled. "And no caffeine, so it won't interfere with sleep."

"I was really worried about that," he said in a droll tone.

"You're probably right," she agreed. "After the day we've had, I don't think either of us has to worry about not sleeping."

Dustin winced as he stretched out his legs.

Concern flooded her. "Does your knee hurt?"

Lowering the mug of tea, Dustin wrapped both hands around the red ceramic before responding. "The sledding didn't make it hurt, if that's what you're asking."

"You mentioned you're not yet back to a hundred percent." Krista kept her tone matter-of-fact. "Will you need more therapy?"

Setting the mug on the end table, Dustin shifted to face her. "Two years ago, when I originally injured my ACL, I had surgery. After seven months of therapy, I was ready to play."

Krista sipped her tea and nodded.

"This last injury wasn't any more severe than the first." He gazed off into the distance for several seconds before refocusing on her. "The difference was, this time I continued to play. I'm done with rehab now. While I'm able to skate, I've been told I'll never get back to where I was before. And if I injure that ACL again, well," he shrugged, "no matter."

"So, you're not going back?" she asked cautiously.

He expelled a breath. "Between you and me, it doesn't look that way."

"Did you...did the team drop you?"

The question hung in the air for several seconds. He shook his head. "Right now, I'm on what's called IR, or injured reserve. It's for players who are expected to be out of action for more than seven days."

"You've been out a lot longer than that," Krista pointed out. "The playoffs were in June."

"It's a minimum of seven days. They're pushing me to go on what's called LTIR, long-term injured reserve. That's for players who are unable to play for ten games or more. If I do that, the team is able to replace me, but my six-year contract terms remain in effect."

"Wow." Krista couldn't keep the surprise from her voice. "That's a sweet deal."

Sensing this was a sensitive area, Krista spoke cautiously as she asked, "Is there a possibility the team doctor got it wrong and you're better than they think?"

"I've seen three of the top specialists in the country. They've all said the same thing and warned that if I try to go back, further injury to that ACL could be, well, crippling."

"I'm sorry." Reaching over, Krista placed a hand on his arm. She couldn't seem to stop herself from touching him. "That had to be difficult news to receive."

"There's no point in me playing if I can't help my team win." Dustin picked up his mug, but made no move to drink. "If I can't play at a high level, I don't want to play at all. Maybe that sounds like an ego thing, but—"

"It doesn't. Our situations aren't really the same, but I do understand how you feel."

Puzzlement filled his gray depths.

"In the modeling world, I'm considered a senior citizen. The big jobs are no longer mine for the taking." Krista's voice thickened with emotion. She paused to clear her throat. "When I go back to the city, I have to accept that my career will be different. The thing is, if I can no longer get the best jobs, I don't know if I want to keep modeling."

Dustin offered an encouraging smile.

"Modeling has been good to me, but I can acknowledge it's not the healthiest environment." Krista shrugged. "I'm not sure it's worth it to me to keep putting myself through it for jobs that don't fulfill me."

"You do understand." Dustin's voice held a kind of wonder.

"I do," she agreed.

"We paid our dues and made it to the top. Now we're both at a crossroads. I think that's why I'm here in Holly Pointe. Not just for R&R, though that's part of it."

Krista inclined her head, curious about where he was going with this.

"I think I came here to come up with a plan, to figure out what's next."

Krista pondered the comment, then gave a slow nod. "I believe, under it all, that's why I chose to come here as well."

"Do you have another career in mind?"

She shook her head. "I don't. I got signed right out of high school, so I didn't go to college. The time never seemed right for more schooling. Which means I don't have the education or really any marketable skills."

"Not true." Dustin set down his mug. He took both of her hands as his steady gaze met and held hers. "Education doesn't have to look the same for everyone. Those years in front of a camera, dealing with all different types of people and situations, gave you a wealth of experience. College can give people more options, sure, and for the record, I don't think there is ever a right or wrong time to go, if that's what you want to do. But don't let the lack of a degree make you feel like less. You're smart, Krista. I could see that even when we were kids. Once you set your mind to something, you can make it happen. I know it."

CHAPTER SEVEN

Krista would have been perfectly happy to spend another couple of hours with Dustin. But when Desz texted that she'd completed her blog and that the cabin door was wide open and ready to welcome her home, Krista reluctantly rose.

She'd thought-hoped—for a good-night kiss from Dustin, but got a hug instead. Still, having him hold her in his arms for those brief seconds had been nearly as nice as a kiss.

The sledding and conversation in front of the fire had rekindled the closeness they'd once shared. Krista realized she liked the man Dustin had become every bit as much as she'd liked the boy he'd once been.

The thought had her smiling as she turned and waved to him. Krista noticed that Dustin remained on the porch until she stepped inside.

"There's the selfie queen." From her position on the sofa, Desz gestured to the bottle and two wineglasses on the coffee table. "Yours is the one on the right."

Krista slipped off her coat. "You're in a good mood."

"I am. I love it when I learn new things, and today was filled with revelations." Desz closed her laptop and tucked it beside her on the sofa. "The blog is in the pipeline, and Lucy, who manages the town website, will be putting up the pics I took of you and Dustin."

Krista dropped into the chair and reached for the wineglass. "I didn't realize you met Lucy."

"I introduced myself to her at the Marketplace." Desz waved a hand. "Enough about me. Let's talk about you."

Krista sipped the wine, then emitted a contented sigh. She did love a good Bordeaux. "Where to begin?"

Her light, teasing tone had Desz grinning.

"So much information to mine." Desz tapped a finger against her lips. "Let's start with the selfie event."

Simply recalling that hour brought a warm rush of pleasure. "It went well, don't you think? Lucy seemed pleased with the response."

"You both did amazing, and you certainly brought in the fans. I got some stellar shots of you and Dustin." Desz's dark eyes sparkled. "I don't know if you're aware, but you're very photogenic."

Krista brought a finger to her lips. "Now that you mention it, someone may have told me that once or twice."

No longer able to sustain the serious expression, Krista laughed. "I can't believe I didn't notice you taking pics."

"You were busy," Desz told her. "Talking to adoring fans and giving them that megawatt smile. Once I had enough good shots, I disappeared into the endless rows of vendors."

"Did you shop for Christmas gifts?"

"Those were bought and shipped before I left the city." Desz waved a dismissive hand. "I was actually in search of blog inspiration."

"And you found one. You said a potter?"

"Miriam Willis. Amazing woman. She has a studio in Jay." Desz took a moment to sip her wine. "She specializes in sculpting really unique flower girls."

"Flower girls?" Krista took another sip of the Bordeaux, savoring the fruity notes. "Like those in weddings?"

"No." Desz laughed. Pulling out her phone, she scrolled, then held it out. "Like these."

Krista took the phone. She studied the images of young females no more than six inches tall with large eyes and pointed ears. "The detail is amazing. Love the flowers in their hair. They remind me of elves."

"That's what I thought, too."

"She's certainly talented, Desz." Krista handed back the phone. "What made her stand out?"

"Remember last summer when I told you I was thinking of taking a pottery class to relieve stress?"

Krista nodded.

"Miriam is not only a potter, but a holistic healer." Desz pocketed the phone. "Trust me when I say I got some excellent info on the tactile benefits of working with clay, as well as additional health tips that will resonate with my highly stressed followers."

"I'm glad it went well." Krista reached over and gave Desz's hand a squeeze. "I felt bad leaving you to fend for yourself."

"Puh-leeze." Desz gave a snort. "You know there's nothing I like better than exploring. And I really appreciate you giving me the time and the quiet to get my blog together."

Krista smiled. "Spending time with Dustin was certainly no hardship."

"What movie did you watch?"

Krista blinked.

"You said you and Dustin were going to grab a beer and watch a movie," Desz reminded her.

"We didn't do either." Krista waved an airy hand. "We ended up drinking hot tea in front of the fire and talking."

A tiny smile played at the corners of Desz's mouth. "I'm sorry. I'm not buying that you and Dustin Bellamy, the Stanley Cup's

MVP and one of the hunkiest men in the NHL, spent the evening enjoying tea and conversation."

"We were cold," Krista began. "We—"

"I can think of plenty of better ways to warm up." Devilment danced in Desz's dark eyes as she pointed her glass toward Krista. "So can you."

Krista laughed. "You're right, but nothing physical happened tonight."

"Nothing?" Desz pressed, clearly not convinced.

Krista's lips curved at the memory of the warm embrace. "He gave me a good-bye hug."

Desz circled a finger in the air. "Whoopee."

Krista laughed again. She didn't bother to explain just how close she'd felt to Dustin in that moment.

"What scintillating topics were on the agenda as you sipped your Earl Grey? Knitting patterns? Or perhaps you exchanged funny cat stories."

Krista rolled her eyes, but had to chuckle.

"We just talked. Nothing super personal. Well, maybe a little personal." Krista had already decided to keep anything Dustin said to her in confidence. "I told him about losing the Shibusa account."

Desz offered an encouraging smile.

Krista expelled a breath. "He listened and was very sweet."

"I'm glad. Seriously."

"Though I love my career and wouldn't trade my years in the spotlight for anything, you and I both know modeling isn't all exotic locations and fancy clothes." Krista lifted her glass, then set it back down without drinking. "There are definite downsides. Gross photographers, rude designers who treat you like an object and being on a diet every day for the last decade."

"But you'll miss it," Desz interjected, her gaze never leaving Krista's face. "The good parts, anyway."

"I will, which is why I'm not rushing this decision. Do I walk away while I'm on top? Or do I hang on, accepting that the prime shoots will go to someone else?"

Desz refilled her wineglass, then held up the bottle with a questioning look.

Krista shook her head. "My career is like a favorite pair of shoes I've outgrown. They gave me a lot of good years, but they've started to pinch."

"Time to shop," Desz quipped.

Krista grinned, then sobered. "I'm not the same young girl I was when I put on those shoes. I've grown and I've changed. My new shoes have to fit the person I am now."

As if understanding that Krista had to get it all out, Desz simply nodded and sipped her wine.

"I'm close to making a decision, but I'm discovering that tossing out the old isn't so easy." Krista offered a wan smile. "The once-favored shoes are in my hands, but I can't seem to let go."

"When you're ready, you will." Desz's soft voice comforted and soothed. "In time, all will be made clear."

Krista met her friend's warm brown eyes. "I hope that's true."

"Did you discuss these concerns with Mr. Foxy?"

"Who?"

"I seem to recall Dustin being named to ESPN's People magazine's Fifteen Foxiest Athletes?"

Krista only chuckled. "In answer to your question, yes. I mentioned I was struggling with the thought of no longer getting the big accounts."

"What did he think you should do?"

"He didn't have an opinion. Like you, he let me talk, but understands it's my decision to make."

Just like the decision he faced was his and his alone.

"When are you seeing him again?"

Krista jolted. She knew there was something she needed to tell Desz. "I nearly forgot. You, me and Dustin are scheduled to go horseback riding tomorrow at two. On Icelandic horses, no less. Unless you have other plans?"

"I don't, and that sounds like a blast." Desz took a long sip of wine and grinned. "I'm always up for a new adventure."

From the cabin's porch, Krista watched the Subaru disappear around a bend in the road. Early this morning, Miriam had texted to invite Desz to her studio to play in the clay. Before Desz left, she promised to be back in plenty of time to go horseback riding.

Though Desz had invited Krista to go with her, Krista knew her friend would get far more out of a one-on-one session with the potter.

The sun and the surprising warmth of the morning had Krista lingering on the porch. She found herself reveling in the unexpected luxury of having nothing on her calendar until two.

Krista turned at the sound of her name and spotted Dustin pulling his front door closed.

"Good morning." She smiled. "You're up early."

"So are you."

Krista wondered if he knew how yummy he looked dressed simply in jeans and a hooded jacket. "Where are you off to?"

"I thought I'd grab breakfast at a place a fan mentioned to me yesterday." Dustin cocked his head. "Have you eaten?"

"Not yet." She hesitated, hoping she hadn't misread the inquiry. "Interested in company?"

"If the company is you, I am."

His response had her smiling. "Let me grab my phone."

"I'll get the Jeep warmed up."

Dustin cast a questioning glance in her direction when she slipped into the passenger seat. "Feeling adventurous today?"

Krista thought of Desz's response. "Always."

"Then we'll give The Back Porch a shot." Dustin's gaze met hers. "The food is supposed to be excellent."

Waving a hand, Krista embraced the moment. "Sounds good to me."

Instead of stopping at one of the Main Street eateries, Dustin continued down the highway that led to Jay. Before they reached the mountain town, Dustin turned down a gravel road.

"Are you sure this person gave you the right directions?" Glancing around, Krista saw nothing but snow flanking both sides of the road. "There isn't any town this way, at least none I know of."

"It isn't a town. It's a house."

"You're taking me to someone's house?"

Dustin chuckled. "Yes and no. The place is called The Back Porch for a reason. The café is located on the back porch of someone's home. The guy who told me about it says the woman who owns it is an incredible cook."

Krista nearly said she wouldn't feel comfortable eating at a stranger's home. Just in time, she remembered Desz and how her friend was always up for something new. "This should be fun."

"I hope so." Dustin pulled onto a long lane that led to a two-story white farmhouse in the distance. "If not, I have the feeling you'll be picking the places to eat from now on."

Dustin parked the Jeep beside two pickups, then he and Krista followed a weathered sign that proclaimed The Back Porch in large, black letters, along with an arrow that pointed toward the back of house.

The porch boasted aluminum-clad windows and siding in need of paint. Two steps led up to a metal storm door that had seen better days.

Reaching around Krista, Dustin opened the door and motioned for her to enter.

She hesitated. "Should we knock? Wait until someone comes to the d—"

"Come in and shut the door behind you," a booming voice called out from inside. "No point heating the outside."

Dustin followed Krista inside, encouraged to discover they weren't the only guests. The space contained four tables, one occupied by three men. Dustin recognized one of the three as Derek Kelly. The other two were strangers.

Derek lifted a hand in greeting to Dustin before his gaze shifted to Krista.

Paying no attention to Derek or his two friends' admiring gazes, Krista chose a table near a window. Dustin worried it might be too cold there until he spotted a small space heater nearby on the floor.

"This is cute." Krista slid her fingers across the blue-and-white-checkered oilcloth that covered the table.

The thought of how it would feel to have those fingers sliding across his skin had Dustin's breath hitching. He forced his attention to the plastic daffodils in the speckled blue pitcher that served as a centerpiece.

"Welcome to The Back Porch. I'm happy you stopped by to see us." The plump, middle-aged woman with tight brown curls set a single-page menu on the table. "My name is Bonnie. I'll be taking care of you today. I'll bring you water, but can I get either of you something else to drink?"

Dustin cast a questioning glance at Krista.

Krista flashed the woman a brilliant smile. "I'd love a cup of coffee."

The woman stared back as if bedazzled. Dustin understood. When Krista smiled, her entire face lit up, and he felt more than a little bedazzled himself.

"Orange juice and coffee for me." Dustin found that his smile didn't garner the same response.

"She seems very efficient." Krista picked up the menu as soon as the woman bustled off. "We better look at this so we're ready to order."

Since the woman had left only one sheet, Krista held it up between them. They studied it in silence for several seconds.

"I'll have the number one." As far as Dustin was concerned, you couldn't go wrong with bacon and eggs.

"Number five for me." Krista set the menu aside and opened her mouth to say more, but then Bonnie appeared.

After setting the drinks on the table, she took their orders, promising the food would be out "in a jiffy."

Dustin took a long drink of the coffee. Not as strong or robust as the blend from the Bean, but still darned good.

Chairs scraped against the speckled linoleum as the three men rose to leave.

When they stopped at the table, Dustin pushed back his chair and rose. "Derek. I was surprised to see you here."

"Not as surprised as I was to see you." Derek chuckled. "The Back Porch is a local place, one of our best-kept secrets."

"Then I won't tell anyone." Dustin gestured to Krista. "Have you met Krista Ankrom?"

"I don't believe—" Derek began.

"My friend and I saw you at the Busy Bean the day we arrived." Krista smiled easily. "Derek, is it?"

"Derek Kelly." Derek gestured to his friends. "This is Zach Adamson and Nick Taylor. Nick will be a new teacher at the high school starting in January. Zach and I are partners in a construction business."

Krista shifted her attention to Nick. "Congratulations on the new position."

"Thanks." Nick smiled back at her, all youthful exuberance. "It's my first job out of college. I get to coach as well as teach."

"Good luck to you." Based on his stature, Dustin decided baseball was likely Nick's sport. Or, if he'd gone to a small school, Nick had probably been one of those guys who participated in all the sports offered.

Such dabbling was foreign to Dustin. Hockey had been his one and only sport from the time he'd put on his first pair of skates at three.

Derek shifted his attention to Dustin. "Quick question. Are you planning to play in the pond hockey game?"

"First I heard of it." Dustin kept his tone offhand.

"You should consider it. It'd be a real boost to the community to have you on the ice." Derek's words tumbled out as he spotted Bonnie approaching with their food. "Kenny has the information. Check with him if you're interested."

"I will." Dustin carefully avoided making any promises.

In seconds, the men were out the door, leaving Krista and Dustin with plates of food and the place to themselves.

Krista cocked her head. "Are you interested in playing?"

"I'm here to figure out next steps." He motioned to her food. "Eat. You don't want your eggs to get cold."

For a second, he thought she might press him for more of an answer, but instead she picked up her fork. They ate in comfortable silence until their plates were nearly empty.

"This was excellent." Krista smiled when Dustin rose to refill their coffee cups. "And I consider myself to be a connoisseur of spinach, mushroom and Havarti egg white omelets."

Dustin lifted the pot sitting on a burner at a coffee station near the door leading inside the house. "My farmhouse breakfast hit the spot."

Once their cups were full, he sat back, ready to relax and fully enjoy Krista's company.

"This was a good choice." Krista smiled at him over the rim of her coffee cup. Setting down her cup, she stabbed the last bite of omelet. "There's this café in the West Village where Desz and I go, specifically for their omelets. This omelet was just as tasty."

Dustin downed the rest of his juice. "Sounds like you and Desz spend a lot of time together."

"As much as we can, considering I travel a lot." Krista set down her fork and dabbed at the corners of her mouth with a paper napkin. "My mom and my aunt are best friends. For me, my girlfriends are my sisters."

Dustin could identify with the sentiment.

"For the past six years, my teammates have been my brothers, my family." Dustin glanced out the window. "Not unusual, I suppose. If I count my college years, I've been away from home for ten years."

"That's how long it's been for me." Krista took a long drink of coffee, her blue eyes cloudy. "When I go back to Ohio, I don't really fit in anymore."

Dustin sipped his coffee and nodded.

"The last time I was home, I'd just gotten back from Australia," Krista said. "There was so much I wanted to tell them. They listened patiently, but really, all they wanted to talk about was my sister-in-law's pregnancy." She expelled a breath. "Nobody cared about the shoot or this really cool coastal drive west of Melbourne where I saw my first koala. That sounds horrible, doesn't it? As if everything has to be about me." Clearly distraught, she waved a hand. "Forget I said anything."

"I'm not going to forget, and it doesn't sound horrible."

"You're just saying that because you're my friend."

"I understand. I do," Dustin insisted at her skeptical look. "Right now, my sister's life is consumed by her husband and boys. Playdates, school carnivals, community stuff. My life is foreign to her. Oh, she feigns interest, but it's not long before we're back to talking about her kids."

"What about your dad? I remember him as a hockey fanatic."

"My dad loves hockey, so we share that passion, but it's difficult for him to understand the pressures of playing in the NHL. He does try."

"I've gotten so I depend on my friends for support."

"That's how it is for me with my teammates." The knowledge that the connection would likely soon be severed was a knife to Dustin's heart.

"You won't stay in touch?"

She seemed to read his mind. Dustin knew the answer to that question was part of the reason he was finding it so difficult to let go.

"Maybe at first." He shrugged. "That will change in time, as I won't be a part of their lives anymore."

"It'll be the same for me." Clouds filled Krista's eyes. "Except for Desz. We'll be friends forever."

"You and I are looking at losing more than just our careers." Dustin shifted his gaze out the window.

When he felt her hand settle on his, Dustin turned and refocused on her.

"While it's a given that our lives will be profoundly different," Krista's blue eyes remained solemn even as her lips curved, "nothing says the next ten years can't be even better."

CHAPTER EIGHT

"The horses are saddled and ready," Sam announced as Dustin and the others reached the stable.

In twenty minutes, the group of six were on horseback and following a trail through the nearby woods. As the path was narrow in this stretch, they were forced to ride single file.

Directly in front of Dustin, Krista rode one of the three Icelandic horses. The pretty roan reminded Dustin of a big pony.

Lucy and Desz had been assigned the other two Icelandic horses. Kevin had told the group that while these horses were small in stature, they were a sturdy, sure-footed breed that wouldn't have any trouble carrying a man.

Desz, on a white horse that Kevin had called a gray, had positioned herself behind Kevin. Sam, despite making it clear he was the older twin—by a whopping two minutes—appeared content to bring up the rear and let his brother lead the group.

It didn't surprise Dustin that Desz began peppering Kevin with questions the second her horse took its first step. Desz appeared to have an insatiable curiosity about practically everything.

In between responding to Desz's endless questions, Kevin

managed to point out a snowy owl high in a tree that they might have missed, as well as two turkey vultures in flight.

His voice carried easily, and Dustin found himself curious if the guy had done any acting.

The men's mother was a big deal, with several Tonys under her belt. Their dad was a top playwright. Dustin wondered, not for the first time, how the brothers ended up in Holly Pointe.

The trail veered out of the woods and onto a dirt road. In the distance, a weathered red barn stood beside a dilapidated farmhouse. The combination of blue sky, white house and red barn created a bucolic picture that drew Dustin's eye.

"Despite the neglect, that makes a pretty picture, don't you think?" Krista shifted in her saddle to smile at him.

Her cheeks were a rosy pink, and her lips reminded him of ripe strawberries. Dark hair spilled from beneath her hat to tumble around her shoulders.

"Very pretty." Dustin spoke without shifting his gaze from Krista. While he appreciated a beautiful woman as much as the next man, he knew there was far more to Krista than a pretty face. She was intelligent and kind, not to mention incredibly sexy.

"Dustin?"

The sound of his name had him blinking.

Concern blanketed Krista's face. "Everything okay?"

"Just taking in the view." He gestured with one hand to the snow-covered scenery. "I'm glad we did this."

"Me, too."

When she smiled, Dustin could have kicked himself. What was with the *we*? He was glad *he* did this.

It wasn't smart to involve her in his life. Not when his was in such upheaval. His phone vibrated in his pocket. Dustin knew who it was without looking. When Dustin hadn't responded to yesterday's texts, Freddie had called earlier this morning.

Dustin had let his agent's call go to voice mail. The fact that

Freddie was being so persistent said something was up. Dustin had the feeling he was calling to tell him team management had decided to write him off.

He understood why. After all, the doctors had deemed him unfit to play. Moving him to LTIR status would allow the team to go over the salary cap by the amount of his salary.

Because he would continue to draw his full salary until his contract ran out in three years, it would appear to be a win-win for both parties.

But Dustin wasn't yet ready to turn his back on hockey and the life he loved.

He slanted a glance at Krista, who now rode beside him on the dirt road.

She was in the midst of her own career crisis. Which meant she didn't need any more on her plate than was already there. Last night in his cabin, it had taken every ounce of his control not to pull her into his arms and kiss her.

At the time, it had felt as if even a kiss would be taking advantage of her vulnerability. He'd told himself that the time wasn't right. Now he wasn't sure it would ever be. They were both facing major, life-changing decisions. Starting a relationship at such a time would make no sense.

Granted, they'd be thrown together again before their time in Holly Pointe was over. Because of their promise to Kenny, that was a given. Other than that, he would make an effort to minimize contact with Krista.

Because one thing he knew—the more he was around Krista, the closer he felt to her and the more he wanted her.

That left him with no choice but to keep his distance.

Krista hoped to have a few minutes to speak with Dustin after the trail ride. She was still in her saddle when Dustin had slipped off his horse, thanked the Johnson brothers, then made his escape, murmuring some vague excuse about pressing business.

Originally, the plan had been for the three of them to drive to Kevin's place together. Dustin had texted shortly before they were to leave that it would work better for him if they drove separately.

Instead of heading straight home, Krista and Desz stopped at Landers Christmas tree farm and picked out a perfectly shaped six-foot fir. They paid extra to have it delivered, and Mr. Landers had assured them he'd have the tree to their cabin by dinnertime.

Krista smiled, recalling how Desz had sweet-talked the older man into agreeing to answer some questions later about Christmas tree farming for her blog.

Since both she and Desz had nothing on the agenda for the rest of the day, they drove downtown after picking out the tree. A Christmas shop in the heart of downtown had everything they wanted and more to decorate the cabin. Krista admitted she went a little crazy on decorations.

Between helping Krista pick out lights and ornaments, Desz managed a mini interview with a glassblower, who was demonstrating her skill at making ornate glass ornaments.

Desz walked out with the woman's card, while Krista carried a box full of tree ornaments and decorations. She marveled at how Desz turned a simple shopping trip into an opportunity. It made her wonder if she was ignoring her own opportunities.

Once back at the cabin, Desz worked on her questions for Mr. Landers.

"Here's what I have so far," Desz announced. "See if you can think of any I missed."

Krista set down her pencil and lifted her gaze from the paper tablet on the table in front of her. "You have my full attention."

"I've done research on the history of Christmas trees, so I don't need to ask him any of those," Desz informed her.

"Understood."

"These are the questions I came up with: What are the best Christmas trees to grow? How do you harvest the trees? How does Christmas tree farming work? When is the most popular time to buy a tree? And any funny stories?" Desz cocked her head.

"Those are good. Before I offer any suggestions, what's going to be the focus of the piece?" Krista remembered how, when she'd first started giving interviews to the media, the agency's PR person had urged her to always find out the focus of an article beforehand.

"Nostalgia." Desz smiled. "More specifically, how sights and smells take us back. I told you how my parents go crazy for Christmas. On the trail ride today, the scent of pine brought wonderful memories flooding back of holidays with my family. Since I usually go home over Christmas, I haven't bothered with a tree since I moved to the city. Now I'm wondering why I never at least hung a pine wreath in my apartment in those weeks leading up to Christmas. You know, to get me in the spirit."

"I feel the same about getting a tree." Krista glanced at the spot where the fir would soon stand. "I'll never go another year without one."

"That's what's good about trips." Desz punctuated the comment with a nod. "You usually learn something about your-self that might never have come up otherwise. Now, back to my list."

"I'm confused about one thing. Why meet with Mr. Landers if nostalgia is the focus?" Krista pulled her brows together. "Do you really need his tree-specific information for the post?"

"My readers like the inside scoop. I'll smatter his specifics through the post, along with information about sights and smells that evoke feelings and memories. I can also tweet his facts and experiences and include a link to my blog," Desz explained.

"Then I think the questions you have are enough to start with. Other questions may come up during the interview."

"I agree." Desz pointed to the pad in front of Krista. "Looks like you've got something of your own going on. Need any help?"

"I'm making a list." Krista resisted the urge to sigh.

"Are you checking it twice?" Desz teased. "Which will it be, naughty or nice? I vote for the former."

Krista laughed and rolled her eyes. "You're good for me, Desz."

Desz grinned, then leaned forward. "Seriously, what's the topic of the list?"

"My strengths," Krista explained. "Along with thoughts on how those strengths might translate into new careers when I'm done modeling."

"Being proactive." Desz offered an approving nod. "Go, Krista, go."

"You're my inspiration." Krista pointed her pencil at Desz. "You're always thinking ahead."

Desz preened. "I like being someone's inspiration."

Krista glanced back at her list. "I wanted a list of twenty, but I'm stuck at seven."

"Read me what you have."

"Okay." Krista took a breath and started at the beginning. "Comfortable in varied social settings. Knowledgeable about fashion. Good at reading people."

Seeing Desz's look of puzzlement, Krista elaborated. "I can tell by the look on a photographer's face whether I'm giving him or her what they want. Since portraying a certain emotion is a big part of what I do, I've gotten good at, well, reading people."

"Makes sense." Desz gestured with one hand. "What else?"

"Comfortable in front of the camera." Krista looked up. "Probably goes without saying, but I thought I should add it anyway."

"Absolutely, you should include it." Desz gave a decisive nod. "You should also add that your warmth comes through in front of a camera. That's not true of everyone."

"You think?" Krista chewed on the pencil.

"I do think." Desz pointed to the paper. "Put it down. What else?"

"Enjoys interacting with people from all walks of life."

"Good. Agree."

Krista smiled. "Cares about charity and community advancement."

Desz's gaze had turned thoughtful. "Continue."

"Loves discovering a person's passion."

"Their passion?" Desz might have kept her tone offhand, but amusement danced in her eyes. "This list is getting more interesting by the second."

"Sorry to disappoint you. There is nothing salacious about it." Krista chuckled. "I believe what someone is passionate about says a lot about them as a person. I've found that talking about pets or art or hobbies is a better way to get to know someone than discussing weather or fashion."

"Passions of the nonsalacious variety. Got it." Desz cocked her head. "What if they're passionate about sex?"

Desz barely dodged the pencil Krista threw at her. "Just kidding."

Krista's smile slipped as she glanced down at the paltry list. "This is all I have."

Instead of rattling off more of Krista's strengths, Desz sat back. "Since this is really about you looking ahead to the future, tell me first how you'd like your future to look."

"I don't understand what you're asking."

"What do you want to do with your downtime? Let's start with where you'd like to live and the pace of that life." Desz studied Krista for a long moment, then prompted, "Big city? Small town? Fast-paced? Slow-paced?"

Krista considered. "Somewhere in between. I love the rush of the city, but I'd like to live somewhere where I can have a house and a yard. Maybe a dog."

"Husband? Kids?" Desz pressed.

Krista hesitated. "Right now, I'm focused on finding a new career that fulfills me. Eventually, I'd like a husband and kids. I guess you could say I'd like to have it all."

"No shame in that." Desz studied her. "I have an aunt and uncle back in Georgia. Sondra reminds me so much of you. She and Uncle Percy are blissfully happy together, but both wanted more than the day-to-day. They made it happen. They were the ones who encouraged me to become an entrepreneur."

Krista found herself intrigued. "What do they do?"

"They have a very successful television variety show. It's devoted to raising Black voices. They feature different Black artists. Usually musicians, but also dancers, poets, really anyone from the arts."

"That sounds amazing." Krista thought for a moment. "I could see myself doing something like that. Only I think I'd focus on artisans like the ones at the Marketplace. Despite being so immensely talented, they get so little recognition."

"You should explore the possibility."

"I don't know the first thing about—"

"Every journey starts with one small step," Desz told her. "The way I look at it, if you're dreaming, you might as well dream big."

Desz had left to meet Mr. Landers by the time Dustin knocked on the door on Friday. Krista had missed seeing her skating stud muffin, as Desz liked to call him.

Dustin had gone radio silent after the trail ride. A few hours ago, Krista had given in and texted him. Ten long minutes later, he'd responded, and they'd finalized plans for tonight's tree lighting. Participating in the lighting together was one of their duties, according to Kenny's list.

"Come in," Krista called. "The door is unlocked."

She remained on the sofa, pulling on a pair of winter-white thigh-high boots she'd purchased new this fall. Wearing them with a leather skirt of the same color created a uniform bottom, while her festive apple-green sweater added a nice pop of color.

The door slowly opened.

"Come in," she said again.

Dustin stepped inside. "What if I'd been a stranger?"

"Then I wouldn't have invited you inside." She gestured with her head toward the window. "I saw you coming up the walk."

His tense expression relaxed. He flashed a smile. "For a second, I thought you might be psychic."

Now that the right boot was in place, Krista shifted her attention to the left. "Sorry, no special skills in that area."

"I saw Desz leave."

Krista made a sound of satisfaction when the boot slid on. She glanced up at Dustin, her tone teasing. "It's reassuring to know that I'm not the only one who looks out the window."

"Busted." His gaze slid from her to the Christmas tree. He pointed. "When did that happen?"

"We picked it out right after the trail ride." Not only was the tree perfectly shaped, the homespun look she and Desz had gone for in choosing decorations complemented the cabin's interior.

The fir boasted buffalo plaid star ornaments, hand-carved wooden snowflakes and tea-dyed cheesecloth ribbon and rusty jingle bell garland. There was even a rattan star tree topper.

"What kind of lights are those?" Dustin stepped to the tree for a closer look.

"Desz had to have those." Krista smiled at the candy cane lights. "I love them, too."

A look of longing filled Dustin's eyes as he fingered a branch of the tree. "I should have gotten a tree."

"Not too late," she told him.

He shrugged.

"Well, if you don't want to get one, you can share ours."

His gaze returned to the tree. "It feels like Christmas in here."

"That's the goal."

After making sure her boots were in place, Krista adjusted her skirt.

"It's a shame to hide those boots beneath that skirt."

Krista swept a hand downward. "See the slit? It allows the boots and a little bit of leg to peek out."

"Nice." His gaze lingered, and Krista found herself growing warm.

"Even if the boots don't show to full advantage, I wanted to wear something a bit more fun and stylish for this evening." She shrugged. "Besides, I know they're under there."

"Now, I know, too."

His smile had heat sliding like warm butter through her veins. Krista had to clear her throat before she found her voice. "How was your day?"

"Tell me about yours first."

As Krista had spent the last few days focusing on her strengths, she realized one of Dustin's was his interest in others. He always seemed genuinely interested in what she had to say.

Krista remembered all too well the people who'd ask her opinion or ask her to explain, then cut her off when she barely got started.

"Desz and I spent most of today at the Marketplace." Raising her hands, palms out, Krista gestured for emphasis. "There is so much talent in that barn."

He inclined his head. "Do you think they're happy they chose to exhibit at Holly Days?"

"I do. And everyone I spoke with was convinced that Selfies with the Stars boosted their profits."

"That's good to hear. I hoped we'd make a difference."

"The clock is ticking. Christmas is two weeks away." She met his questioning gaze with a firm one of her own. "We need to do more to help Holly Days succeed."

He rocked back on his heels. "What do you have in mind?"

"We talked before how Kenny's list of required duties was bare-bones. It's time to brainstorm additional ways we can bring visitors to Holly Pointe. We've got to move on this. We can't put it off any longer."

He studied her, then gave a reluctant nod.

"Selfies with the Stars went great. Check that off. Tonight, we light the Christmas tree. We'll check that off. All that's left is walking the red carpet the night of the Mistletoe Ball." She met his gaze. "It's not enough, Dustin. It's just not enough."

"You're right. We'll brainstorm tonight." He held out a hand. "Right now, we need to go."

Krista took his hand. As she let him pull her to her feet, all thoughts of Holly Days fled in the warmth of his touch. Did he realize, she wondered, how good he smelled? Being so close to him now had her noticing all sorts of things. Like how his charcoal sweater made his gray eyes pop. And how his hair shone like spun gold in the glow of the lights.

She was sorely tempted to slide her fingers into the wavy strands. Even more tempted to press her lips against his mouth and let herself drown in his kisses.

"Are you ready?"

Krista jerked her mind back from the salacious daydream forming in her head. "I am. We should go."

Grabbing her ivory cashmere coat, Krista followed Dustin outside. The tree lighting tonight was business. As was any discussion of their future duties as the *Holly*wood Stars.

As she caught the faint hint of his cologne, Krista felt her lips curve. As far as she knew, there was no law against mixing business with a little pleasure.

CHAPTER NINE

"We were smart to walk." Krista glanced around as they neared the business district. "I don't think we'd have found a parking spot anywhere close."

Dustin glanced down at her heeled boots. "My only concern is you walking this distance in those."

He gestured with his free hand. Krista had slipped her hand around his other arm for better stability on the occasionally slippery walkway.

"It feels like I grew up in heels." She laughed, a pleasant sound that eased his worry. "I could walk in these for days. Desz is the same."

"Speaking of Desz, where is she tonight?" Dustin had expected Desz to be there when he'd stopped by the cabin to pick up Krista.

"I'm not sure." Krista's brows pulled together. "She said she had a surprise and would catch up with me later."

Dustin scanned the crowded sidewalks ahead. "Kenny has to be pleased with this turnout."

"The number of people here tonight reminds me of how it used to be." Krista expelled a happy breath.

Many things reminded him of before. Like now, walking to the tree lighting with her. "Would you like to pick up a coffee?"

"I see where you're going with this."

"Ah, where is that?"

"While we're there, we can inform Kenny that we're looking for other ways to use our *Holly*wood Stars status to promote Holly Days." Krista tapped a perfectly manicured fingernail against her temple. "Great minds think alike."

"I take it that's a yes for coffee."

Her fingers tightened around his arm as she shot him a brilliant smile. "You know me so well."

They reached the doors of the Busy Bean, but had to wait while a group of teens filed out. At the last second, instead of stepping inside, Dustin took her by the hand and pulled her down the sidewalk, moving fast.

"What—" she began.

"Just come." Once they reached the alley, he made the turn into it.

This was no normal alley. Well-lit and paved, it boasted ribbons of light in red, green and blue strands overhead. Metal sculptures decorated the walls of the brick buildings on both sides.

They weren't alone either. This particular alley served as a popular connecting walkway between the businesses on Main Street and the ones on the next block.

As everyone else was headed toward Main Street, it felt as if he and Krista were swimming upstream.

Dustin saw a few of the men's gazes lingering on Krista as they passed. He didn't blame them. She was a beautiful woman. What they didn't understand was that her beauty was more than skin-deep.

"Does it bother you when men stare?" he heard himself ask.

"I've gotten to the point I barely notice." She chuckled. "Which is probably why there hasn't been anyone special in my life for a long time. I need to start paying attention."

"I imagine finding the time to date was difficult with your schedule."

"That's one reason," she admitted.

"What's another?"

The light in her eyes dimmed.

"A lot of men only want to be with me because of how I look." Her laugh held no humor. "You'd be surprised at the number of middle-aged men who troll the runway scene, successful, powerful men who want to show their friends and colleagues that they're desirable to young, beautiful women."

She spoke of her beauty as fact.

Dustin wondered if she was aware of how the creamy white of her coat provided a vivid contrast to her dark hair and green sweater. Then he realized that of course she did. Knowing that kind of stuff was her business.

He slowed to a stop before they reached the end of the alley. "Surely you found a few who were sincere in ten years?"

Dustin wasn't sure why he pressed the issue.

"If you're asking if I have a guy waiting for me back in New York, the answer is no." Her tone was matter-of-fact. "There have been guys I liked, who I enjoyed being with, but none of those relationships went the distance. Sometimes it was me, sometimes them. Whatever the reason, it just wasn't right. What about you? Are you in a serious relationship?"

Dustin opened his mouth, then shut it. He'd nearly said he wouldn't be having the thoughts he was having about her if he was serious about someone else.

"I'm not in a relationship right now, serious or otherwise." He shrugged. "Like you, I've dated, but I've never found anyone that I cared enough about to get serious. And never enough to put them above my career."

"You didn't think you could have both?"

"Some guys do. There were men on my team who are married, some with kids." Dustin cleared his throat. "I needed to be the best. Relationships take time. Hockey was my priority. I'm sure it sounds—"

"It sounds to me as if you and I have been traveling down similar paths. There were many who attempted to make me feel bad because I made it clear my career took priority."

"You didn't care enough about them to try to make it work."

"You didn't either," she pointed out, then shifted gears. "Tell me why we bypassed the Busy Bean."

"You noticed?"

She laughed. "You practically dragged me down the street. Of course I noticed."

"I spotted a couple of ESPN reporters speaking with Norma." Dustin clenched his jaw, then forced himself to relax.

"You're used to speaking with the media." Krista spoke in a low tone as two couples brushed past them.

"I am. But I came to Holly Pointe to stay out of the spotlight, not attract attention."

A softness filled her eyes. "Then Kenny roped you into being a *Holly*wood Star."

"I made the choice," he spoke firmly. "I love Holly Pointe. I wanted to help."

Krista offered an encouraging smile.

"I'm concerned about drawing the wrong kind of publicity. When Kenny put media interviews on his list, I was worried, but I assumed it would be smaller, local newspapers." Dustin shook his head. "I know some tenacious journalists, but I never thought anyone would find me in Holly Pointe. Any attention on me will bring my injury and impending retirement to light and take the focus off Holly Days."

Dustin blew out a breath. "Even though I've been out of action for months now, I'm still very much in the public eye. Sports journalists continue to speculate about my future. That's why I'm steering clear of them and—"

The phone in his pocket buzzed. After glancing at the screen, he sent the call to voice mail. "And not speaking with my agent, no matter how many times he calls and texts."

Admitting it made him feel like a coward. He waited for Krista to tell him he needed to face his fears and—

Her fingers closed around his arm. "Take the time you need to decide. Don't rush the process."

Dustin looked up and found himself drowning in her liquid blue depths. Only then did he realize that keeping his distance from her would be impossible.

Seeing that Dustin still wasn't ready to go back to Main Street and risk running into the reporters, Krista paused when they reached the end of the alley and scanned for a place to lie low.

Pawsibilities called to Krista the instant she saw the words Pet Couture below the shop's name and the gorgeous white tree with pet-friendly ornaments in the window. She insisted they go inside.

The shop was a plethora of delights, from the *Lady and the Tramp* Bon Appetit display of pet dishes and gourmet foods, to the stuffed felines sporting adorable sweaters, called Cats on Parade. One even wore a tutu.

Krista didn't know much about cats, other than several of her friends owned them, but she didn't think a real kitty would appreciate being dressed in tule.

"Hi, may I help you find something?" The woman, tall with short dark hair and glasses, stopped abruptly.

"Krista Ankrom." The woman shifted her gaze, and her smile widened. "And Dustin Bellamy. I can't tell you how honored I am to have our *Holly*wood Stars in my shop."

"Ms.—" Krista began.

"Everyone just calls me Marley."

"Well, Marley, your shop is absolutely adorable." As Krista shifted her gaze to the Cats on Parade display, something clicked in her head.

The shop owner smiled at Dustin when he picked up a dog collar in neon green covered in hand-stitched paw prints. "Do you have a dog?"

"Not right now," he told her, setting down the collar. "But when I was growing up, we always had a dog. Once I'm settled, I plan to get one."

"Marley." Krista drew the woman's attention back to her. "Dustin and I are looking at ways we can help promote Holly Days."

With that introduction, Krista laid out the vision forming in her head.

By the time she and Dustin walked out of the store, Krista had Marley's card and had promised to be in touch.

"A fashion show called Catwalk?" Dustin shook his head once they were back on the sidewalk.

She shot him a glinting glance.

He held up his hands. "Just kidding. It's a fabulous idea. I can see how it would play to the media and to the tourists. Especially with you involved."

"I can see it so clearly. Locals dressed in clothing from stores in Holly Pointe or handmade knitted items from Marketplace vendors, walking or carrying a dog or cat decked out in Marley's pet fashions down a runway at the barns." Krista had to pause for breath. "There are so many *pawsibilities*."

Dustin groaned. "That is so lame."

"I think it's clever." She smiled. "Anyway, we could even borrow animals from the local shelter for a Catwalk."

She spread her hands as if picturing a marquee.

Dustin brought his hands together for two solid claps. "I'm

impressed. One glance around the shop was all it took for your creativity to surge and for you to come up with the perfect event. You're savvy enough to know that a model hosting a pet fashion show is not only clever, but will attract more attention to these businesses. I'm impressed."

"I can see it in my mind." Krista's excitement grew. She continued to extol the benefits as they stepped back onto Main Street.

They'd barely gone half a block when they spotted Lucy and Kevin. Even if the couple hadn't been right in front of them, Kevin would have been difficult to miss.

The stuffed reindeer antlers on his head were covered in Christmas lights that pulsed to a frantic beat. Lucy sported a necklace of bright bulbs in red, green, yellow and blue that slowly winked on and off.

"Where are your antlers?" Dustin called out to Lucy as they approached.

"They didn't go with my red hat." Lucy lifted a gloved hand to her knitted cap and grinned.

Krista had the feeling the hat was an excuse. Not too many people could carry off antlers on steroids.

"There was a time when this one wouldn't think of putting on a necklace like this, much less wear it out in public." Kevin's arm slid around her waist, pulling her close and planting a kiss on her temple.

"Truer words." Lucy laughed. "My mom isn't into holiday stuff, so we never did much. Kevin and Sam are both crazy about Christmas."

Lucy slanted a glance at Kevin and smiled. "Those two have been easing me over to the dark, er, Christmas side since we were kids."

Krista could see that Lucy didn't mind the slow slide into holiday glee. Maybe because Lucy's feelings for Kevin went beyond friendship. That was obvious, at least to Krista.

"Where are you guys headed?" Lucy asked.

"We've been wandering, getting a feel for the crowd before the tree lighting and singalong." Dustin shrugged. "No specific destination."

Krista touched Dustin's arm. "If we're going to see it all, we better start strolling."

Dustin smiled. "Lead the way."

After saying good-bye to Kevin and Lucy, they walked for a distance before Krista gestured with one hand to the festive scene spread out before them. Main Street had been barricaded off for the evening, allowing vendors to set up in the street. "There is so much to see and do. I'm not sure which way to go first."

Dustin gestured to a couple of food trucks parked at the curb, as well as numerous small stands offering their own specialties. "Looks like finding something to eat won't be a problem."

"I'm not really hungry." She shifted to look at him. "But if you want something…"

He shook his head. "I'm okay with eating later, once we get the tree lighting and singing out of the way."

"Looking forward to it that much, are you?" She chuckled, then the laughter died at the pained look on his face. "Dustin? What is it?"

"I'm a horrible singer." He lifted a hand. "Before you say I'm exaggerating, I'm not. My mother, who thinks her kids walk on water, told me once in church that it was okay if I just mouthed the words."

Krista's eyes widened. "She did not."

"I never sing in public. Heck, I don't even sing in the shower." He shifted from one foot to the other. "Trust me. If I lead the caroling, everyone will run screaming into the night."

"While I'm reserving judgment on how bad you really are, I'll take you at your word."

"Appreciated."

"What if you do the countdown on lighting the tree, and I lead the singing?" She smiled. "You can sing or simply mouth the words. Your choice."

He grinned. "I knew I liked you."

"Good." She leaned over and brushed his mouth with hers. "Because I like you, too."

CHAPTER TEN

While Dustin might not enjoy singing, Krista had to stop herself from joining in with the carolers strolling down the street. She couldn't remember the last time she'd been this happy.

All around her, bells jingled and people greeted each other with "Merry Christmas" or "Happy Holly Days." They found Kenny, er, Santa in front of the courthouse on a thronelike chair of crushed red velvet.

Krista sucked in a breath. She tugged Dustin's arm. "Look."

There was Desz, an adorable Santa's elf complete with striped tights, a green hat that matched her dress and pointy-toed shoes.

From what Krista observed, Desz's job appeared to be to usher children to Santa while keeping the line moving.

Santa was a popular attraction with a long line of children waiting to whisper their Christmas wishes. With them stood parents poised to capture pictures of the momentous occasion.

Catching Krista's eye, Desz mouthed, "Surprise!"

Krista waved and smiled. She should have known she'd find Desz in the middle of the action.

It was apparent Desz had no time to talk, so she and Dustin continued down Main Street. They passed a life-size igloo made out of plastic milk cartons that had been set up for kids to explore. Up ahead, Krista spotted a face-painting station and several artists doing caricatures.

"I don't remember Holly Days having all these events when we were kids," Krista said to Dustin.

"I don't either." Dustin shook his head. "A lot of this is new, or new since we quit coming. It appears the committee is doing whatever necessary to make Holly Days more appealing to visitors."

"They have to in order to compete."

Dustin scanned the snow-laden landscape. "It'd be so much easier if the weather was warmer."

"But not nearly as special."

Dustin inclined his head.

"It wouldn't seem like Christmas without snow." Krista lifted her face and let her tongue catch a single snowflake. When she shifted her gaze back to Dustin, she found him staring.

His gaze remained on her face. "I agree. This feels like Christmas to me."

"It'll seem even more like Christmas with a penguin on your cheek." She grabbed his hand and pulled him over to one of the face painters.

His sputtering stopped before they reached the artist, who appeared starstruck and introduced herself as Cheryl Dunham.

"This is wonderful," Cheryl gushed. "Having a *Holly*wood Star with my design on his cheek is a dream come true."

Krista gestured to Dustin to have a seat. "He wants the skating penguin."

"That will be perfect." Cheryl reached for her paints. "I can even add a hockey stick if you'd like."

"Sounds good." Dustin took a seat in her chair. "Your designs are amazing."

While Cheryl worked on Dustin, the woman's partner drew Santa ringing a bell on Krista's cheek.

Krista clasped her gloved hands together when they finished. "You're both so talented."

"Amazing." Dustin's gaze remained on the mirror for several seconds longer before he rose and turned to Cheryl. "How much do we owe you?"

"Not one cent," the woman decreed, and her partner nodded. "It was our pleasure."

Dustin looked back at the line forming. "The next few customers are on me."

Cheryl gazed down at the large bill he'd pressed into her hand. "This is a lot—"

He winked. "Tell the kids it's from Santa."

Krista would have liked to have stayed longer, but the line continued to grow. She and Dustin had barely gone three steps before the next two customers were seated.

"Looks like we spurred some business." Krista sighed happily.

"They're talented. They'd have done okay without us."

"Sometimes talent is enough." Krista thought of her modeling career. "Sometimes it's breaks coupled with the talent."

Dustin slanted a sideways glance at her. "Talent and hard work coupled with the right place, right time and a whole lot of luck."

The wind kicked up, and Krista wrapped the cashmere scarf more tightly around her neck. "I made a list this week."

"What kind of list?"

"A list of my strengths." She expelled a breath. "Which I hope will help me as I look for a new career."

"Did you come up with any options?"

Krista pulled her brows together, recalling Desz's aunt and uncle. "I like being in front of the camera, and I'd like to use that comfort to do something that raises up artists, that gives them a shot at their own success." Krista thought of Marley at Pawsibilities and Cheryl with her talent for caricatures. "What we're trying to do as *Holly*wood Stars."

Dustin gave her hand a squeeze. "I can see you being successful at something like that. Then again, I believe you'd be good at whatever you set your mind to. You have so many marketable talents, much more than you give yourself credit for. My only advice is, when you look at possible careers, choose something that will make you happy."

For the next hour, Krista wandered through the fun and festive atmosphere, made even more enjoyable with Dustin at her side. In no hurry, they stopped to talk or take selfies with strangers.

"It's nearly time." Dustin gestured toward the twenty-foot fir in the town square.

Others must have realized the hour for the lighting was fast approaching, as she and Dustin found themselves pushed along in a tide of people toward the magnificent tree.

"It's pretty, even without the lights." Krista held tight to Dustin's arm as they skirted around the people stationed around the tree's perimeter. They kept moving until they reached an area that had been cordoned off, then climbed the two steps to the raised platform, where Kenny waited.

Kenny, still dressed as Santa, rushed to them. "You two are doing a wonderful job. I hear it from everyone."

"I'm surprised there was time for anyone to tell you anything."

Krista gave him a hug, and he offered a delighted, "Ho-ho-ho."

She stepped back, smiling at him. "Every time I looked, the line for Santa stretched all the way to the street."

"Norma and our daughters keep me informed." Kenny shoved a list into their hands. "Sorry I didn't get this to you sooner. This is the order of the Christmas carols."

"There's only three." Krista glanced at him in surprise. "I thought there would be more."

"People tend to have short attention spans." Kenny's chuckle turned into another "ho-ho-ho" that made Krista smile. "If you see people start to wander off after the first carol, don't worry. Happens every year."

Dustin shoved his hands into his pockets. "Good to know."

"Oh, and if you see a bunch of reporters, it's probably because I sent out press releases, not just locally or even to Burlington and Albany. I swung for the fences and sent them to NYC and Boston and even Montreal, since they're cities with lots of big hockey fans." Kenny clapped Dustin on the back. "Good luck and enjoy."

A muscle in Dustin's jaw jumped.

Krista smiled. "Oh, Kenny, just so you know…"

Kenny, hand on the rail, whirled at the sound of her voice. "Is there a problem?"

"No problem," she assured him. "Just an update. Dustin will introduce us, then do the countdown. I'll lead the singing. We felt it would work better that way."

"You're the stars," was all Kenny said.

"It's time," Dustin told Krista.

When Krista turned to follow Kenny down the steps, Dustin touched her arm. "Stay."

She cocked her head.

"We're their *Holly*wood Stars. For some, this will be their first glimpse of us." Dustin's expression remained serious. "They'll want to see both of us onstage."

"You're right." Krista took the scarf around her neck and expertly arranged the plaid cashmere into a bow.

A roar went up from the crowd when she and Dustin moved to center stage. Like her fellow *Holly*wood Star, Krista smiled broadly and waved.

"Thank you all for coming tonight. I'm Dustin Bellamy." He waited for the cheers to subside before gesturing to Krista. "This is the always lovely Krista Ankrom."

Krista was touched that her cheers were nearly as loud as Dustin's had been.

"We're here tonight because of our love for Holly Pointe. We want to bring attention to everything the fabulous Holly Days has to offer. You may not realize that both Krista and I came to Holly Pointe every year with our families while we were growing up." Dustin's tone turned serious. "I've been all over the world, and I can tell you that there's no better place to spend Christmas than right here."

The cheers rang out again.

Krista leaned close to the microphone. "There's nothing like the lighting of a Christmas tree to give you that warm holiday feeling."

Dustin smiled at her, and she realized there was nothing like a man you cared about smiling at you to prompt that feeling as well.

"As many of you know, I'm a team player." He grinned at the crowd's response. "Which means I'd like us to do the countdown to the lighting together."

The roar in response seemed to shake the treetops.

"We'll start at ten."

Krista watched his gaze slide across the people standing there, the couples, families and singles. It was as if he was personally inviting each of them to share his enjoyment of Holly Days.

Bringing the revelers into the countdown had been a brilliant move. Dustin might not know it, but he had a real knack in front of an audience.

"Ten," Dustin shouted into the mic. "Nine."

By eight, the crowd and Dustin were in perfect sync. Krista's role in this segment of the evening was to nod to Ginny Blain, a local woman who'd been chosen to throw the switch that would light up the tree.

"One," the crowd screamed.

Krista gave a nod.

The tree exploded in a brilliant array of lights that filled the night sky. Cheers, whistles and applause rang out.

Krista's heart became a warm sweet mass as memories flooded back. Happy tears filled her eyes as she remembered how her dad used to sling his arm over her shoulders and kiss her temple when the lights flashed on. Her mother would squeeze her hand, and her mom's eyes would be as bright as the star atop the huge tree.

Her brother always tried to act cool, like seeing the tree lighting up the sky was no big deal. Still, Tommy always cheered as loudly as the rest of them. Even after he'd reached his teens, he'd never missed the tree lighting.

Such wonderful memories, she thought, all centered here in Holly Pointe.

"Stellar job, Bellamy," Krista said to Dustin and was rewarded with a blinding flash of smile.

"You're up," he told her.

"This is one of the moments I always looked forward to every year," Krista said into the microphone. As Dustin had only moments before, she let her gaze sweep the crowd. "The holiday season wouldn't be complete without getting together with a group of friends to sing some much-loved carols. Whether you have a voice like a pop star or a frog, I encourage you to sing out. Let the spirit of Christmas embrace you."

"We'll be doing three songs this evening." Dustin leaned in close to the mic. "These should be ones you know, so don't try to pretend you don't know the words."

Laughter rippled through the assembly.

They made a good team, Krista realized. Each of them contributing to the two segments had offered variety and kept the crowd's interest.

"We'll begin with a classic." Krista nodded to the person handling the sound system. The familiar melody of "Silent Night" wafted out.

The blending of voices raised in song had Krista shivering. Beside her, Dustin wasn't just mouthing the words, he was singing softly.

She understood. It was impossible not to join in.

They did two more carols, and when the last refrain ended, a hush fell over the crowd.

Krista brought a hand to her chest. "Amazing. I'm sure I'm not the only one who felt the magic."

Dustin leaned forward. "This isn't the end of the evening's festivities. Eat, drink and visit as many of the amazing vendors here tonight as possible."

He touched a finger to his face. "For fellow hockey fans, Cheryl at Face Art painted this skating penguin with a hockey stick on my cheek. I'll be posting to Instagram and Twitter tonight. Be sure and tag me so I can see yours. When you do, use the hashtag #hollydays so I don't miss it."

Smart, Krista thought. Get as many people as possible involved in spreading the Holly Days message.

"There are more *Holly*wood Stars activities coming to the Barns at Grace Hollow. Which means you'll get to see more of me and this guy." Krista jerked a thumb in Dustin's direction, and the crowd roared. "Make sure to check the Holly Pointe website for details. And tell all your friends."

"We look forward to seeing all of you again real soon." Dustin slid an arm around her shoulders.

Cameras flashed, and Krista had no doubt that Dustin wouldn't be the only one tagged on social media. She wasn't used to having her picture taken without looking one hundred percent camera ready, but she told herself this was for a good cause.

Dustin extended a hand to her as she stepped from the raised stage. Even though the steps were perfectly dry, she appreciated the gentlemanly gesture.

They hadn't taken two steps before a woman stepped in front of them.

She flashed a press pass. "I'm Alice Roth from *The Barre-Montpelier Times Argus*. I'd love to speak with you about Holly Days and your roles as *Holly*wood Stars. I just have a couple questions. I won't keep you long."

Krista glanced at Dustin, who gave a barely perceptible nod. "We have a few minutes."

"Let's take this inside the Busy Bean." Dustin offered Alice the smile that always made Krista's heart flip-flop. "We can grab a cup of something hot while we talk."

The woman, somewhere in her mid-fifties with a thick thatch of gray hair, nodded. "Perfect."

As they walked toward the coffee shop, Dustin slanted Krista a glance, and with the barest flicker of her eyelashes, she let him know they were on the same wavelength.

They'd stick to promoting Holly Days. Whatever personal information they chose to share would be up to each of them.

CHAPTER ELEVEN

Dustin had looked forward to strolling the downtown area with Krista once their duties ended. But he told himself that this reporter from a community little more than an hour away had the power to draw people to Holly Days with her words.

Norma waved to them when they stepped through the door, pointing to a table near the back sporting a reserved sign. "You can sit here. Tell me what you want. I'll bring it out."

She gestured with her head to the long line at the counter, where two teenagers moved expertly to fill orders. "I don't want you to have to wait."

"The sign on the table says reserved," Dustin pointed out.

"For you and Krista." Norma smiled at Alice. "And the media."

After giving Norma their order, they moved to the table. While they waited for the drinks, Dustin took charge of the conversation.

"How long have you worked for the *Times Argus?*" he asked the woman.

"Nearly twenty years." Alice gave a little laugh. "It sounds so long when I say it out loud."

"You must enjoy your work to have stayed that long." Krista

leaned forward, her eyes bright with interest. "What do you like most about it?"

"The constant change. There are always new stories. And how we report the news continues to evolve. We're much more involved online." Alice smiled her thanks when Norma arrived with three cups of hot cocoa, complete with candy cane stir sticks. She reached inside her pocket for her credit card. "My treat."

"On the house." Norma waved away the payment. "We're happy to have you here."

The older woman hurried off before Alice could protest.

The reporter smiled and gestured to Norma's retreating back. "That was nice of her."

"Holly Pointe is an amazing community." Dustin hoped the comment would segue into a discussion about Holly Days.

"The people here are wonderful."

Dustin silently applauded Krista's enthusiasm.

Krista continued when Alice didn't respond right away. "They are just one of the reasons Holly Days is so popular. Singles, couples, families love to come to a community that makes them feel at home and welcome. And there's so much to do here."

Dustin resisted the urge to give Krista a high five.

Alice took a sip of her cocoa. "Tell me how a model and a hockey player ended up as *Holly*wood Stars."

When Krista slanted him a sideways glance and passed the puck, Dustin took it down the ice.

"Krista and I grew up celebrating Christmas in Holly Pointe." Dustin wrapped his fingers around his ceramic mug. "When Kenny asked me to be a *Holly*wood Star, I was eager for the chance to promote a community that means so much to me."

"It was the same for me." Krista filled the momentary silence. "I felt honored Kenny would ask."

Alice tapped her pen against the tabletop. "You two already knew each other."

"All the families who came here every year knew each other." Dustin gestured toward Krista. "Like Krista said, Holly Days is all about family and building connections."

"When was the last time you were in Holly Pointe?"

Krista paused, bringing a long, elegant finger to her lips. "Ten years."

"Close to that for me, too." It was exactly the same for Dustin, but if he repeated Krista's answer, Alice might draw some erroneous conclusion about the timing when it was truly only a coincidence that they both showed up this year.

Alice's gaze had turned eagle-sharp. "After a decade away, why come back now?"

Dustin wasn't about to get into anything concerning his injury, but it was such a part of why he was here that he had to search hard for another reason to explain his presence.

Krista slid effortlessly into the void.

"For the first time in ten years, I didn't have a shoot over Christmas. My last project of the year ended earlier this month." Krista paused to take a sip of cocoa, setting the cup down with a sigh of pleasure. "My family already had plans. I guess I was feeling nostalgic."

Alice shifted her focus to Dustin while making notes.

"Last-minute decision for me." Dustin kept his tone offhand. "When you have a schedule that keeps you traveling, you need a relaxing place to recharge."

The second the words left his mouth, Dustin realized he'd opened a door to the topic of his injury by mentioning his former busy schedule.

A spark flared in Alice's eyes. "Speaking of your sched—"

"When I described Holly Pointe to my friend Desz Presley, she was like, 'Yes, I really want to go there and see this wonderful place for myself.'" Krista smiled brightly. "Desz is now in full agreement that there isn't a better place to enjoy the holidays with a friend or family than Holly Pointe."

Alice straightened. "Desz Presley, the blogger, is here in Holly Pointe?"

Krista nodded.

Alice immediately reached into her bag and pulled out a card. "Would you have her contact me? I'd love to interview her."

"I'd be happy to." Krista slipped the card into her coat pocket, pleased by Alice's interest in Desz and her blog.

"Thank you." Alice shifted her attention to Dustin. Behind her silver-rimmed spectacles, the reporter's dark eyes turned sharp and assessing. "I understand there are pond hockey games scheduled. Will you be playing?"

"I'm glad that pond hockey is still so popular around here." Dustin's voice remained easy. "We're anticipating a big turnout. Whether you're five or fifteen or fifty, you can get some time on the ice and have fun doing it."

"Will you be playing?" Alice asked again.

"We're still finalizing our *Holly*wood Stars schedule." Dustin gestured with one hand toward Krista. "Any appearance by one, or both, of us will be reported on the town's website."

Dustin silently congratulated himself for sidestepping her question.

"I understand you've been undergoing rehab for an injury." Alice glanced down at her notes, but Dustin saw by the excited look in her eyes that the pretense was only for form. "You haven't played in more than six months, not since the Stanley Cup Finals in June. There's speculation your injury was more severe than initially reported.

"I don't mind answering sports questions when that's the purpose of the interview." With great effort, Dustin kept his tone even. "When you asked for a few minutes of our time, you specifically stated your article's focus was on Holly Pointe and Holly Days, not—"

"It's all news," Alice interrupted. "People want to—"

"I agreed to be a *Holly*wood Star to promote a community I

love." Though his posture remained easy, steel now edged his voice. "That's the reason I'm sitting across from you now."

He offered her a smile that he feared wouldn't quite reach his eyes. "If you want to talk hockey, I'm afraid you'll have to get in line behind reporters from the NHL Network, NBCSN and Fox Sports."

When he pushed back his chair and stood, indicating the interview was over, Alice asked quickly, "Would you mind if I got a couple of pictures?"

Krista glanced at Dustin, and he gave her a barely perceptible nod.

"Sure," Krista rose. "Outside or in?"

"In, I think." Alice pulled out her phone. "Outside, we may have issues with lighting and the public wanting to get involved."

Krista glanced around the coffee shop and pointed to an area off to the side where a huge metal reindeer stood. "The light would be best over there."

With an experienced eye, Alice studied the area and nodded. "I agree."

Two poses and a burst of shots later, Alice strode out of the coffee shop.

By tacit agreement, Dustin and Krista took their time putting on their coats, wanting to be sure Alice was well on her way.

"You handled that interview like a pro," he told Krista. "I hope she'll come through with some good stuff about Holly Days."

"I'm not super familiar with her paper, but Montpelier is an easy drive to Holly Pointe, perfect for anyone to impulsively come up and enjoy the festivities." Krista looped her scarf carelessly around her neck. "I was surprised you picked the Bean to speak with her."

Zipping his coat, Dustin cast her a curious glance.

"The reporters that were here earlier…"

"My sense is they were only in here to see if Kenny would tell them where they could find me." Dustin chuckled. "If I had to guess, I'd say they've moved to searching the bars for me."

"At least they'd be honest about what they were after." Krista's blue eyes turned dark. "Alice told us she wanted to talk about Holly Days, but she really only wanted information on your injury."

"Let's give her the benefit of the doubt. She was most likely sent here to report on Holly Days." Dustin stuffed some money into the tip jar, then held the door open for Krista. "But she's a reporter. She saw an opportunity and took it."

"Tried to take it," Krista pointed out. "You shut her down."

He smiled as they strode out into an evening filled with tiny snowflakes. "If she'd been a seasoned sports reporter, she'd have ignored the pushback and driven even harder to provoke a news-worthy comment."

Krista shook her head. "Why can't they leave you alone?"

"You and I both know how the media works. Ferreting out information and disseminating it is their job." Dustin shrugged.

After a moment, Krista chuckled.

"What?"

"I was just thinking how quickly the media coverage would escalate if you played in the pond hockey game." Krista's lips continued to curve upward. "Having you on the ice would bring the reporters and the public out in droves."

"Which is exactly why I'm considering it." The admission surprised Dustin nearly as much as it surprised her.

"You are?" Krista stopped on the walkway and turned to face him. Snowflakes covered her dark hair and lashes.

"You know how you had the Catwalk epiphany when you walked into Pawsibilities?"

She slowly nodded.

"Playing in the pond hockey game has been in the back of my mind since it was first mentioned."

"I know you miss being on the ice…" She spoke slowly, her gaze never leaving his face.

"I was thinking, what if I did a hockey clinic for kids in the morning before the game?"

"That would certainly bring parents with hockey-loving children to Holly Pointe." Krista inclined her head. "Would you do the clinic and then skate in the game? Or just do the clinic?"

"I'm thinking both." Dustin blew out a breath.

"You're not worried that the media will be focused on your injury rather than on Holly Days?"

"A little bit, but I like that the game and Holly Days will also get lots of free publicity." He slung an arm around her shoulders. "In fact, I'm liking this idea more and more."

"Kenny is going to go crazy when you tell him."

"Just like he will when you mention the Catwalk idea." Dustin smiled. "We make a dynamite team."

She grinned back at him. "We're setting the bar high for future *Holly*wood Stars."

"Assuming Holly Days continues."

"Oh, ye of little faith." Krista pointed to him, then to herself. "This dynamite team is going to make sure that Holly Days continues for many years to come."

By the time they reached the cabins, snow fell steadily. Lights shone in her cabin, telling Krista that Desz was home.

"You've got snowflakes in your hair." Dustin studied her for a long moment, his eyes like gray smoke in the dim light. "You need a hat."

She brought a finger to her lips, then nodded. "A Santa hat would have been a festive touch."

Just as she hoped, his gaze remained on her mouth. "I was thinking more along the lines of it keeping you dry and warm."

Her breath now came in short little puffs, but from his nearness, not the chill. Krista kept her gaze fixed on him. They'd danced around this attraction long enough. "I'm never cold, not when you're with me."

A slow smile lifted his lips.

Krista fought a shiver of anticipation and prayed Desz didn't choose this moment to fling open the door.

Taking a step forward, Dustin wrapped his arms lightly around her. "I've been wanting to do this since I first saw you again."

Finally, blessedly, his mouth covered hers.

Krista settled her hands on his shoulders and savored the delicious, wonderful taste of him. He scattered kisses across her face, her lips and her neck before returning to her mouth.

This kiss had her knees going weak as desire pulsed through every inch of her body. She slid her fingers into his hair and poured all the feelings she had for him into the kiss.

Someone—her? him? did it even matter?—gave a soft moan.

Seized with the urge to crawl inside him, Krista settled for kissing him as if this was her last chance. The last time she would kiss him, the last opportunity to show him how much she cared, how much she loved him.

The thought brought her up short and had her stepping back. Dustin released her immediately. She might have fallen had he not reached out to steady her.

Dropping his hold on her once she'd regained her footing, he raked a hand through his hair and emitted a soft chuckle. "Wow. Just…wow."

She smiled and kept her tone light as she fought to quell the surging emotions. "You were right. We do make a dynamite team."

CHAPTER TWELVE

Krista groaned when her phone's wakeup song sounded. "Why did I ever agree to bake cookies at this hour?"

The sound of her voice had Desz opening the door and popping her head inside. "You didn't sign us up, I did. And it's going to be a blast."

Pushing herself upright, Krista sniffed the air. "Did you start the coffee?"

"While still in my jammies. Priorities, girlfriend." Desz appeared way too chipper, considering it had been past midnight when they'd finally gone to bed. "I also texted Alice. She and I are meeting later today."

"Wow, she works fast."

"I like a person who knows what she wants and goes after it." Desz smiled. "Alice and her daughters are huge fans of my blog."

"Who isn't?"

"Good point." Desz glanced at her wrist. "Better get a move on, Ankrom, or there'll be no time for coffee."

"There's always time for coffee," Krista shot back.

Still, knowing Desz was right about limited time had Krista

dressing in a hurry, quickly applying her makeup and pulling her hair into a twist.

At last ready to face the day, she poured herself a cup of the steaming brew and inhaled deeply before taking a drink.

A knock at the door had her calling out, "Come in," before realizing she shouldn't just assume it was Dustin stopping by.

Still, the instant she heard the *clop* of boots on the hardwood, she knew it was him.

Leaning back against the counter, she held up her mug. "We have coffee."

He glanced around the kitchen. "Where's Desz?"

"I'm not sure," Krista advised, "but she's up and going."

"I could use some coffee."

Turning, she grabbed the cup she'd set out, then poured him some.

"Thanks." His fingers brushed hers as he took the mug.

Electricity skittered up Krista's arm, bringing the memory of last night's kisses front and center.

"I saw your lights on." He took a long drink of coffee, then smiled. "I was wondering if you had any plans this morning."

"We're baking cookies at the Candy Cane Christmas House," Desz answered his question as she breezed into the room. "Then I'm meeting with Alice, leaving Krista to fend for herself."

"You could come bake cookies with us." Krista was surprised to realize just how much she hoped he'd say yes.

A doubtful expression crossed his face. "I've eaten my share of Christmas cookies, but I don't believe I've ever made any."

Impulsively, Krista reached out and took his hand. Her heart skipped a beat when he wrapped his fingers around hers. "Please. It'll be fun."

He studied their joined hands, then brought them up and pressed a kiss on the top of hers. "As long as I can eat, as well as bake, count me in."

~

The Candy Cane Christmas House was a massive Victorian home with towers, turrets and a wraparound porch. Dustin vaguely recalled his mom and sister coming here to wrap gifts for underprivileged children and soldiers.

The owner of the house, Mary Pierson, a regal-looking woman with snow-white hair and warm blue eyes, greeted them at the door. She took his hands when he introduced himself. "You're Dianna's son."

Dustin couldn't hide his surprise. "You remember my mother?"

"She's unforgettable." After giving his hands a squeeze, Mary stepped back. "Every year, she'd come to the gift-wrapping. She had talent for it, too. Your sister, well, Ashleigh was still learning, but her help was also very much appreciated."

Dustin suddenly became aware that, in the distance between the foyer and the front parlor, they'd managed to lose Desz to a woman who was off in a corner putting together a gingerbread house.

Overhead, instrumental Christmas music added to the home's holiday charm.

Mary's gaze slid between him and Krista. "Before we start baking, let me just say how very much I appreciate all you're doing to promote Holly Days."

"We're really enjoying it." Dustin glanced in the direction of what he assumed was the kitchen. "Cookie-making sounds intriguing, but I need to warn you that I'm the most basic of beginners."

"I imagine when you put on your first pair of skates, you didn't have an arsenal of dekes." Mary smiled. "You've got to start somewhere. Come now, let me show you the kitchen and get you started."

Krista glanced in Desz's direction.

Desz had leaned close and was intently watching as Ginny Blain, the woman who'd flipped the switch on the tree last night, raised the walls of the gingerbread house.

"Your friend can join us or not." Mary waved an airy hand. "I imagine Ginny is attempting to convince her to attend the how-to class on gingerbread houses that she's teaching this afternoon."

"If that's the case, and if Desz has the time, she'll be there." Krista smiled. "She loves learning new things."

When Mary stopped to speak briefly with another woman about an upcoming ornament workshop, Krista leaned close to Dustin.

"What's a deke?" she whispered.

Dustin smiled. Mary's casual use of the hockey term had told him the older woman was a fan of the game. "It's a way of getting around a defenseman. It involves stickhandling moves, changes in direction and speed. This is very simplistic, but think of it as feinting like you're going to go in one direction, but you go the other."

"I learned something new today." She tossed her head with pride as they followed Mary into the kitchen. "Now, it's your turn."

Dustin hadn't planned on baking cookies today, but he liked eating them, and he wanted to be with Krista. When Mary asked if they preferred to work as a team, she got an enthusiastic yes from both of them.

Desz made a brief appearance to ask if it was okay if she stuck with observing Ginny. Once Mary gave her blessing and after giving Krista a quick hug, Desz headed back to the parlor.

Placing a hand on his arm, Krista pointed to the space on the tabletop earmarked as theirs. "The first step is to mix the ingredients together, then refrigerate the dough for at least an hour. Mary already did that for us."

Dustin wondered if she knew how her eyes glowed when she

was excited. Her red lips matched her sweater. He nodded and had to force himself to look away. Either that or kiss her.

Later, he promised himself. If she was willing. And from the looks she kept casting his way, she had more than cookie-making on her mind, too.

They worked together on shaping the cookies, then putting them in the oven. Instead of making them wait out the baking and cooling time, Mary brought over a dozen sugar cookies shaped in stars for them to frost.

Dustin glanced down at the star-shaped cookies. "Blue stars were my favorite as a kid."

Krista pointed to the bottles of food coloring. "Then let's go with blue for the main color and white for the edging."

Mary set two empty squeeze bottles before them, one bigger than the other. "For the icing."

"The thicker icing—the white—is what we'll use to create an edge around the cookie." Krista handed him a bowl. "That edge will hold in the blue, thinner icing. You can start by whisking the ingredients together."

In the end, Krista did the white edging, and he did the blue center. They then each picked up a toothpick to spread the blue icing over any bare patches.

All went well until they got to cookie number thirteen, and their toothpicks decided to have a hockey battle on the field of blue. By the time, Dustin scored by crossing the white edge with his toothpick, they were both laughing.

Dustin pointed to the messed-up top and the blue oozing out over the sides where the frosting edge had been breached. "We have to eat this one."

"No choice," Krista agreed.

They each popped half into their mouths as they surveyed the other cookies.

Krista glanced up at him. "Sprinkles?"

"What are stars without sprinkles?"

They added the multicolored bits of sugar to the cookies, then stepped back to admire them.

"Now they have to sit for twenty-four hours," Krista announced.

Dustin's smile faded. "Are you serious?"

"Krista's right. They need to sit so the icing can harden." Mary, who'd been making the rounds in the room, placed a hand on Dustin's shoulder. "Still, I think you should both sample your finished masterpieces."

Mary gestured to some brightly wrapped plates of cookies on a side table. "I have a dozen cookies for you to take home. While they won't be the ones you made yourself, I believe you'll enjoy them."

"Thanks for letting us come and do this, Mary." Krista gave the woman a hug. "I haven't done any baking for years. I'd forgotten how much I enjoyed it."

"Yes, thanks," Dustin echoed. "I had fun."

"Come again anytime." Mary chuckled. "Though I imagine Kenny will be keeping you two pretty busy."

She might have said more, but her phone began to play "Jingle Bells." Mary's expression lit up like a Christmas tree. "Excuse me. That's my granddaughter Faith's ringtone."

After Mary hurried off, Dustin picked up one star, splitting it in half and handing one side to Krista and keeping the other for himself.

Krista held up a hand and counted down on her fingers. "Three. Two. One."

Dustin bit into the cookie. He instantly realized the value of letting the icing harden, as the blue frosting squished in his mouth. Still, the taste couldn't be beat.

"You've got a little blue right here." Krista stepped forward and brushed his lip with her thumb, wiping the extra icing from his mouth.

His breath hitched when her tongue flicked the icing off her thumb, her gaze never leaving his face.

"Krista." He stepped forward, his voice husky and low.

"Dustin." On her lips, his name sounded like a caress.

"I haven't been able to stop thinking about last night." Though the only other people in the kitchen were two elderly women on the other side of the room, Dustin's voice remained soft as a whisper. He took her hand and stroked her palm with his thumb.

"I haven't either." She cocked her head. "What do you say we go to your place and…"

She didn't finish the thought, didn't need to finish. As Dustin gazed into her baby blues, he saw the same want and need he felt reflected back at him. "What about Desz?"

"She's got an interview with Alice sometime this afternoon. I'm not sure what time."

Her phone rang before she could say anything more. She accepted the call while leaving the phone on the counter where she'd set it earlier.

"I'm putting you on speaker, Desz." Krista continued to wipe icing off her fingers with a damp rag. "Why are you calling? I'm in the next room."

"We're putting on the roof." Desz spoke in a hurried tone. "And I wasn't sure where you and Dustin were in the cookie—"

"We're actually done and ready to leave."

Desz expelled an audible breath. "I want to stay and finish this, then interview Mary and Ginny before I take the ginger-bread house class. The class will end about the time I need to drive to meet with Alice. Alice said she knows this adorable Thai restaurant in Jay, so we thought we'd meet there, but I don't want to leave you alone or without a car, so if me being gone until this evening will be a problem, you just say the word and—"

"Desz." Krista jumped in when her friend paused for breath. "It's all good, really. Dustin and I have a couple of things to do, one of which is to conference with Kenny about some *Holly*wood

Stars stuff. Dustin has a car, so don't worry about me being stranded. Stay out as long as you like."

"You really don't mind?" Relief filled Desz's voice. "I know we came here together—"

"I'll say it one more time—I really don't mind. Learn a lot, and most of all, have fun. After all, that's why we're here."

"You have fun, too."

"Oh, I definitely intend to." Krista turned to Dustin and winked before ending the call with a happy, "Ciao."

CHAPTER THIRTEEN

After leaving the plate of cookies with Desz, Krista stepped through the front door of the Candy Cane Christmas House into bright sunshine.

With Dustin by her side, she strolled the two miles to the cabin. Desire shimmered in the air as they talked of possible ways that they could promote Holly Days. By the time they reached Dustin's cabin, anticipation had reached a fever pitch.

Dustin waited until they were inside the cabin, the door shut and locked behind them, to pull her in for a kiss.

Wrapping her arms around his neck, she returned the kiss, wishing there weren't all these layers of clothes between them.

"I've missed you." Dustin breathed the words, resting his head against the top of hers when they came up for air.

"We were just together last night." Krista let her fingers slide into his hair, reveling in the feel of the soft, wavy strands.

"I'm talking about the years we've been apart. I believe part of me has missed you since the day my family left Holly Pointe so abruptly ten years ago." His gaze searched her face. "I never thought I'd see you again."

"This, being with you now, is an unexpected gift." Krista laid her head against his chest, drawing comfort from his nearness. "I've never cared about anyone as much as I cared for you."

He said nothing, simply brushed a kiss across the top of her hair.

"I realize that probably sounds ridiculous," she began.

"It doesn't." Dustin cleared his throat. "It's how I feel about you."

She lifted her gaze and offered him a tremulous smile.

"I want to make love with you, Krista. I want that in the worst way." Impatiently, he pushed back a lock of hair that fell across his forehead. "But I can't promise more than what we'll have here in Holly Pointe. My life is in turmoil right now—"

"You forget that mine is just as unsettled." She pulled back just enough to look into his eyes. "If this time is all we have, I'm okay with that."

"You're sure?" His gaze remained steady, but the muscle jumping in his jaw told her how much effort it was taking for him to hold back.

Raising a hand, she laid her palm against his cheek. "I want you, Dustin. Just as much as you want me. Maybe more."

He suddenly grinned, a boyish smile that melted her heart. "Not possible."

They fell into each other's arms. Krista had been kissed before, but never—no, never—like this. Not where she felt as if their souls were coming joyfully together after a long separation. Short, sweet kisses were followed by long, dreamy ones. Then kisses that set her blood on fire.

They stumbled toward the bedroom, their mouths melded together. Clothing fell like windswept rain onto the hardwood floor. A coat here, a pair of shoes there. Clothes—hers and his —formed a scattered trail from the front door to the bedroom.

"You have protection?" Krista put a hand on his arm at the edge of the bed. It was a little late to ask, but Krista was finding rational thought difficult with Dustin's now-naked body pressed against hers. "I'm on the Pill, but—"

"I have protection," he confirmed, brushing a dark strand of hair back from her face with the side of his hand. "You have nothing to worry about."

Krista knew that wasn't true. She had plenty to worry about, beginning with how was she going to live with a broken heart once she and Dustin went their separate ways.

She shoved aside the worries. For now, she would rejoice. All was right in her world. Dustin was here with her now. That's all that mattered.

"Enough talk," she proclaimed, her voice quivering with pent-up desire.

He grinned. "Impatient much?"

Planting her hands flat against the wide breadth of his chest, Krista leaned in and kissed him, openmouthed. She let everything slip away and simply gave in to the moment.

The world was still spinning like an out-of-control Tilt-A-Whirl when Dustin took her hand and pulled her down on the bed with him.

While his hands skimmed up her body to stroke, brush and linger, his mouth returned to hers over and over. He seemed to sense exactly where she liked to be touched.

It felt amazingly good to be with him in this way. To have the chance to show him with her actions just how much she cared.

Krista planted a kiss at the base of his neck, his skin salty beneath her lips. When his hand flattened against her lower back, drawing her up against the length of his body, she moaned, a low sound of want and need.

He rolled away, his hand diving inside the drawer of the bedside stand and coming out with a foil packet. Then, thankfully, blessedly, he returned to her, kissing her with reckless abandon while his magic fingers sent vibrations of desire coursing through every inch of her body.

"Now," she ordered, the word coming out on a tear. "Now."

Just as she suspected, they fit together perfectly.

He tried to go slow, but his need was too great, her desire too strong.

The beat of her heart mingled with his as he raced with her. Pulling his face down with her free hand, she gave him a ferocious kiss, then came apart in his arms.

His own release quickly followed. Breathing hard, he eased to the side.

Krista felt a chill, but then he looped his arms around her and pulled her close. She snuggled against him as he planted kisses on her cheeks, her hair and her mouth.

As Krista met his eyes, love—of the strong, forever kind—blew through her. No, she thought, it wasn't going to be easy to say good-bye. But she was determined to savor each moment.

He studied her for several seconds, his steady gaze shooting tingles down her spine. "Tell me what you're thinking."

It took several erratic heartbeats for her to find her voice. Smiling, she trailed a finger down his cheek. "I'm thinking I'm glad we have all afternoon."

Four days later, Krista's Catwalk event took center stage in the Marketplace.

"Mary Pierson wondered if she and Ginny Blain could exchange alpaca ruanas?" Desz glanced at her clipboard. "She thinks her red and black looks better on Ginny."

"Tell her that's fine." While Krista would walk the runway—she was, after all, one of the *Holly*wood Stars that spectators cramming the Marketplace had come to see—she was also the event coordinator.

She had lots of help. Dustin, Desz, Norma and Lucy had all put in the hours to help her pull off the event on short notice.

Then there were the vendors, all of them eager to have their items on display during the Catwalk.

Marley from Pawsibilities had been a godsend, taking over the tasks of dressing the rescue pets and assigning each to their "person." That had left Krista and her crew to focus on outfitting the humans while showcasing as many vendor products as possible.

Desz touched her shoulder. "Do you need anything else?"

Krista smiled. "I believe we're nearly ready to go. Dustin—"

"Has delivered the animals from the shelter. Marley and her crew are getting them dressed even as we speak." Dustin grinned at her. "She told me the potbellied pig has your name on it, darlin'"

Krista wasn't sure if he was teasing or not. The *darlin'* coupled with the twinkle in his eye said that was likely the case. "A pig?"

"Lulu is pretty and, ah, large. Marley has a dress with red poppies and a tulle skirt that she's going to put on her." Dustin paused. "Well, attempt to put on her."

Krista did a double blink. "You expect me to walk a pig down the catwalk?"

"Take it up with Marley if you have concerns. Not my call." Dustin lifted his hands. "But think of the publicity."

"That's all I've been thinking of." Krista turned to Desz. "You should get dressed and ready."

"Do I get a pig, too?" Desz asked Dustin.

"Marley is coordinating the animals," Dustin reminded her.

"I'm going to see if I can have a pig." Desz hurried off.

"I can handle whatever else needs to be done." Dustin ran a hand down Krista's arm. "Take a few minutes for yourself."

Krista tapped a pencil against the clipboard and glanced around the large room, which was standing room only. "I want everything to be perfect."

"It's going to be as perfect as it can be with cats, pigs and dogs." His droll tone made her laugh.

"Your idea to list all the sponsors' booth locations on poster boards around the Marketplace was brilliant," Krista told him.

"As was yours to run the hockey clinics every morning," he volleyed back. Dustin glanced at the clock on the wall. "You have ten minutes to change."

"Piece of cake." Krista wanted to kiss him, but conscious of the eyes on them, she settled for giving his arm a squeeze.

"I can't wait to see what you're wearing."

"I'd have done a private fashion show for you, but there hasn't been time." She lowered her voice to a confidential whisper. "Maybe tonight, I can put it on, and you can take it off."

Desire turned his gray eyes darker. "That's a plan I can get behind."

To build anticipation for the Catwalk, Krista had asked a reporter from the local paper to visit different shops with her while she'd searched for the perfect dress. The reporter had agreed not to reveal her ultimate choice so that people would have to attend the event to see what she wore.

Krista had once done something similar to help promote a designer friend during New York Fashion Week. The mystery had generated a lot of buzz for her friend's business. Hopefully, it would work well in Holly Pointe, too.

The dress she'd model today had come from One More Time, a vintage-clothing store in Holly Pointe.

The boutique's business was mostly online, although they supplied costumes to theater departments in the region, as well as sold individual pieces to free-spirited individuals who wanted something unique to wear.

The moment she'd seen the simple 1950s red wool swing dress, she'd known it would be perfect for a holiday fashion show. The snug-fitting top and narrow, high waistline fit her slender frame like it had been made for her.

Her lips quirked upward. When she'd chosen the dress, she

hadn't realized the color would coordinate perfectly with what her pig would be wearing.

As soon as Krista arrived backstage, Lucy ushered her into a small private area to change. Krista might be used to changing in the middle of activity, but she appreciated the privacy.

After fluffing her hair with her fingertips, Krista applied bright red lipstick and gazed at herself in the mirror. She'd worry later about how she'd stroll the runway with a pig.

Right now, she had a show to emcee.

Krista found Lulu to be adorable in her outfit and more than a little stubborn. She followed Lulu onto the catwalk as the last ones to walk the runway. The flashes from cameras and the oohs and aahs from the audience told her Lulu was a hit.

It felt good to walk a runway again, even a makeshift one that was barely four feet high. Krista let Lulu take the lead. The pig moved from one side of the catwalk to the other, sniffing and snorting while ignoring the spectators.

Once Krista reached the end of the catwalk, she paused for more pictures, then turned back, giving a tug on Lulu's leash. The pig didn't move.

Lulu continued to sniff, only now her snout was up, and she was sniffing the air like a hound who'd caught a scent.

Krista kept smiling and surreptitiously tugging.

Out of the corner of her eye, she saw Kevin, wearing a sweater sporting the image of a gingerbread man with the words Bite Me across the front. He pushed his way through the crowd that lined both sides of the catwalk, concern etched on his face.

Behind her, she heard Dustin's footsteps coming down the catwalk, moving fast.

She wanted to tell them both not to worry, that she was a

professional, and no potbellied pig was going to get the best of her.

Then Lulu located the source of the smell. Near the end of the runway, a guy stood beside his girlfriend, munching on a gyro while scrolling through messages on his phone. The man appeared to have no clue that an eighty-pound pig had his sandwich in her crosshairs.

Without warning, Lulu lunged.

Several women at the end of the runway screamed and scattered.

Krista held tight to the short leash hooked to Lulu's harness. No way was she letting a pig dive into the crowd. Not only could Lulu hurt someone, she might injure herself.

Unable to gain purchase with her heels, Krista kicked them off, all the while keeping tight tension on the leash. Even without the shoes, Krista slid forward.

Until, apparently deciding that getting to the sandwich was too much work, Lulu abruptly turned, and the tension on the leash released.

Krista stumbled back and might have fallen, but Dustin was there, scooping her up in his arms, even managing to grab the leash of a now-docile Lulu.

The crowd erupted in cheers.

"You've still got the moves, Bellamy," someone in the crowd called out.

Krista's kiss on Dustin's cheek had cameras flashing.

Dustin grinned, held her for another second, then let her down with obvious reluctance. He remained close while Krista put her shoes back on, balancing against him with one hand.

Lulu, now the picture of pig innocence, simply looked around as if wondering what the fuss was all about.

Though her heart beat an erratic rhythm, Krista took the microphone Lucy handed her with a steady hand. She smiled and gestured to Dustin. "Let's give a round of applause to the man with all the right moves, my fellow *Holly*wood Star, Dustin Bellamy."

Applause and whistles rang out.

Dustin leaned close to the mic. "I'd like us to show some love to Krista Ankrom. This *Holly*wood Star not only organized and oversaw the first Holly Days Catwalk, she put a petulant pig in her place to make the event a success."

Krista slipped her arm through Dustin's and drank in the applause. Then she let her gaze pan the audience. "We appreciate each and every one of you. As well as all the volunteers who helped bring this event together."

"We encourage you to visit the amazing artists in this room." Dustin leaned close again to share the microphone. "When you're done here, head over to downtown and check out all the amazing stores."

"For the young ones, and those young at heart, Santa is waiting in front of the courthouse to hear your Christmas wishes," Krista reminded the audience. "Thanks again for coming."

The decision to have Kenny downtown rather than in the Marketplace had been strategic. Everyone who came to watch the Catwalk was already here, so the vendors had an advantage. The goal was to spread the wealth by encouraging these shoppers to also check out the downtown shops.

Reporters pressed around the stage, clamoring for an interview with her and Dustin, but Krista only smiled, waved and, giving Lulu's leash a tug, walked off in the other direction with Dustin.

CHAPTER FOURTEEN

After relaxing for a few minutes and enjoying a glass of wine backstage, Krista and Dustin decided to be visible in the vendor area. They'd made it down only one aisle when Desz's voice rang out over the din of the shoppers. "Over here."

They wove their way in that direction to find Desz standing in front of a booth where a woman with long, silver hair pulled back in a clasp sat at a spinning wheel.

The woman briefly looked up. "A pleasure to meet you."

"Hello." Krista shifted her gaze back to the wheel.

"That's amazing work." Dustin frowned in concentration. "What kind of fur is that?"

"Meet Indigo Miller," Desz said. "She spins dog fur into yarn. Then she triple-washes the finished skeins and—"

"I do both dog and cat fur," Indigo clarified. "What I'm spinning now is from a Husky. As I was telling your friend here, I often combine the pet fur with a support fiber, because that helps a small quantity of fur become a usable amount of yarn. It also increases the breathability."

"It's amazing." Desz beamed at the woman. "Indigo has this

super-interesting story about how she got involved in this business. I want to feature her on my blog."

"I'm sure your readers will find her story fascinating," Krista told Desz.

"I'd love to add a video of the two of you speaking with her." Desz's expression turned pleading. "Please?"

"I don't have any questions prepared—" Krista began.

Desz immediately waved aside the protest. "All you need to do is ask any questions that come to mind that you think viewers and readers would ask."

"You don't need to do this if you don't want," Indigo assured her. "But I wouldn't mind the publicity."

"We can do this." Dustin glanced at Krista.

What was it about his use of the word *we* that had her heart fluttering?

Pulling her gaze from his, Krista turned to Indigo. "I'm fascinated, so, sure, we'll do it."

"Forget I'm here," Desz told the three of them. "I can edit out any bloopers. Starting video now."

Instead of looking at the woman or jumping in with questions, Dustin faced Desz's phone. "Here in Holly Pointe, Vermont, artisans from all over converge on this Christmas community to show off their talents during the town's annual Holly Days."

Krista immediately understood how he planned to play this, and it was brilliant. Keeping her face partially toward the phone, she directed her comment to Dustin. "Living in New York City provides me with plenty of shopping opportunities."

Dustin smiled. "You do love shopping."

"Guilty." Krista held up a hand and laughed. "Which is why I'm loving this Marketplace."

She forgot Desz and the camera as she and Dustin bantered back and forth, then brought Indigo into the discussion. They asked questions that everyone would want to know, but when

Dustin sat down at the loom, the encounter turned into something special.

He didn't seem to mind that he was awkward and unsure or that he got tangled in the yarn, making them all dissolve into laughter.

That led to Indigo relaying stories about her early mishaps with poodle fur.

"If you have a pet you've lost, or one who's still around, this is a way to commemorate your love for your fur baby." Krista turned to Dustin. "Everyone simply has to come and check out Indigo at her Sleeping Dogs Twine booth."

Dustin gestured widely with his arm. "As well as all the other artisans here."

Krista cocked her head and shot Dustin a flirty smile. "You got pretty good at the loom. Can I count on a homemade skein of yarn from you this year?"

Dustin slung an arm around her shoulders. "I guess you'll have to wait and see."

Krista faced the camera. "If you want to give a unique and wonderful gift to someone special in your life, Holly Days is the place to be. Dustin and I look forward to seeing you all here in beautiful Holly Pointe."

Desz lowered the camera. "That was fabulous. You guys are naturals in front of the camera."

Slanting a glance at Krista, Dustin smiled. "You were amazing."

"Backatcha." Krista chuckled. "There were times I forgot that Desz was videoing. It was fun."

"Thank you." Indigo's gaze shifted from Krista to Dustin. "This extra publicity really means a lot to me and to all the other artists here."

"We're happy to do it," Dustin assured her.

"Well, it looks like a crowd is gathering." Krista tugged at

Dustin's hand. "Wouldn't want to get in the way of potential customers."

She and Dustin followed Desz off to one side.

Desz gripped Krista's hand, her gaze sliding from her friend to Dustin. "That was very cool. You two have this natural repartee. I felt like I was watching pros in action."

"You are too kind," Krista began, embarrassed by Desz's effusive praise.

"I'm not." Desz lifted her phone. "Trust me, the final results will speak for themselves. I'm heading home now to start editing."

While Desz worked on her laptop, Krista changed out of the swing dress. The red color reminded her of Lulu and made her think about how things could so easily have gone horribly wrong.

Krista pointed to the wine bottle on the table. "Can I have some of that?"

Without looking up, Desz smiled. "Absolutely."

After pouring herself a glass, Krista took a seat at the table. She gestured with the hand holding the glass to the screen. "Can I see?"

"Not until it's done." Desz shifted her focus, giving Krista her full attention. "I can tell you the video interview is amazing."

"So says the woman who won't even give me a sneak peek." As Krista sipped her wine, she felt the last of the tension ease from her shoulders. "I guess I'll have to take your word."

"I'm a perfectionist," Desz admitted without apology. "Remember when you were making your list, and I told you how you have a natural warmth in front of the camera?"

Krista smiled. "It was a lovely compliment."

"Well, it's a fact and very evident in this video." Desz paused. "What surprised me is Dustin possesses that same quality."

"Why should that surprise you?" Krista found herself indignant on Dustin's behalf. "He's a personable guy."

Desz shrugged. "Personable doesn't always translate, but in his case, it does. Not to mention you two have this off-the-charts chemistry and a comfortable interviewing style. That's what makes this video so spectacular."

"Spectacular, eh?" Krista's lips curved as she took another sip. "Maybe I really should give the artisan-interview thing a shot."

Ever since she and Desz had spoken about her future, Krista kept circling back to that option in her mind.

Desz studied her thoughtfully.

"Talking to Indigo, discovering what she does and why she does it, was fun." Krista absently brought the wineglass to her lips, but then lowered it. "Just like when I spoke with Marley at Pawsibilities. Not only did I learn new things, but I was helping someone and having fun doing it."

"Having fun, enjoying our life's work, is the point. Or it should be anyway." Desz studied the screen in front of her, then made some changes.

"When we get back to New York, I'd like you to give me your aunt and uncle's contact information."

Desz looked up in surprise.

"If you think they'd be willing to speak with me about the variety show they do, that is." Krista set down her glass. "I have some contacts in the city who might also prove helpful, but I'd—"

"They'd love to speak with you and share what they've learned." Desz's voice vibrated with excitement. "You're seriously thinking of doing this?"

"I'm seriously exploring the pawsibility, ah, possibility."

Desz gave a snort of laughter.

"I believe I could be happy doing what we discussed." Krista found Desz's excitement contagious. "I've got money saved to use for start-up costs and to tide me over initially. I can also keep modeling if need be to bring in additional revenue."

Admiration shone in Desz's dark eyes. "You've given this more thought."

"The idea is coming together, but I need more information to determine if it's workable."

"It's a good plan." Desz glanced at her laptop screen.

"We can talk more later." Krista waved an airy hand. "You're busy, and Dustin asked me to stop over. I told him I needed to check with you. I can stay and chat with you, or—"

"Go." Desz pointed to the door. "Leave me to my work."

The flash of Desz's smile belied her grumpy words, and Krista chuckled as she gathered her jacket for the quick trip next door.

Dustin sat in front of the fire, sipping a beer and waiting for his phone to ring. So far, no call or text from Krista. Then again, he hadn't been home all that long.

He could understand Krista not wanting to abandon her friend, but he hoped, really hoped, she'd be able to get away.

They'd been in close proximity all evening, but there hadn't been an opportunity for anything nonwork-related. Still, tonight's event had been enjoyable.

By the time he'd made his way to the last booth in the last aisle, Dustin had felt as if he'd spoken with a thousand artisans. The crazy thing was, conversation had come easy, and he'd enjoyed learning about how different pieces of art were created.

He'd even learned from one vendor that Vermont had the highest number of artists per capita of any state.

The knock at the door had his head jerking up. He hoped it was Krista, but when he reached the door, he stopped short. "Who's there?"

"It's me."

Dustin smiled and opened the door.

"Who did you think I was?" she asked, offering him a bright smile as he helped her remove her jacket.

"I hadn't heard from you, so a tenacious reporter was my first thought." The people in Holly Pointe had done a good job at respecting his and Krista's privacy by not giving out where they were staying, but Dustin knew it wouldn't be all that difficult for someone to follow them home.

"No reporter." She hung her jacket on the coat tree. "Just me."

When she turned, he saw she'd exchanged her dress for leggings and a sweater.

"You didn't give me a chance to take it off."

"Take what off? Oh." She laughed. "You mean the dress. I had to ditch it. It reminded me too much of Lulu."

Tying the pig to her dress didn't make sense, but Dustin let the comment go.

Krista was here. With him. That's what mattered.

He rested his hands on her waist and tugged her close, pleased when her arms twined around his neck. "Desz didn't mind you leaving?"

"She was busy editing the video."

He inhaled the intoxicating scent of her perfume. "How did it turn out?"

"She said fabulous, but she wouldn't let me see it." Krista shrugged. "Not until it's perfect."

"I'd like to see it."

"Absolutely." Krista gave him a quick hug, then stepped back. "It's positively frigid out there. Let's sit in front of the fire."

She grabbed his hand and pulled him along.

He shook his head. "I must be doing something wrong if being close to me doesn't keep you warm."

Krista dropped to sit on the sofa he'd positioned to face the hearth and patted the spot beside her.

Dustin sat and slipped an arm around her shoulders. "Now

this, you," Dustin clarified, "is what my night was missing."

She tilted her head, and the firelight made her blue eyes mysterious and her dark hair look like polished walnut. "I'm sorry I didn't call or text. Desz gave me the go-ahead, and I shot out the door."

"I'm just glad you're here." He played with a lock of her hair. "I enjoyed today, far more than I imagined."

She leaned her head against his shoulder. "Other than the misadventures of Lulu, the event was a smashing success."

He planted a kiss on her temple. "Lulu met her match in you."

Krista smiled. "I had a little help from my fellow *Holly*wood Star."

"I was happy to be of service."

"Best of all, tonight's event helped me see what my next career could be."

"You want to run a pig farm?"

She swatted him with the back of her hand. "I'm being serious."

"Sorry. Couldn't resist." Fighting a twinge of envy, Dustin offered an encouraging smile. "What did you come up with?"

"Desz's aunt and uncle have this television show devoted to raising Black voices. They feature all different kinds of artists." Krista paused. "I can see myself doing something similar, only with a focus on artisans like those at the Marketplace. Despite being very talented, these artists get so little recognition."

"I agree about the recognition and the talent." He pulled his brows together as he mulled over the idea. "Where would you begin researching doing something like that?"

"Desz said her aunt and uncle would be happy to speak with me. I'll find out how they got started." Krista's gaze turned thoughtful. "I've got contacts in New York that I can also mine for information."

"Would you set the show in New York?"

"I don't know." Krista gave a little laugh. "I don't think so, but maybe. Desz's aunt and uncle's show is based out of Nashville. The production costs would definitely be lower there."

"I'm impressed." Admiration coursed through Dustin. "I'm also not surprised. I knew once you figured out what you wanted to do, you'd make it happen. And now look at you." Dustin let out a small laugh. "You're moving down your next career track, while I'm still stuck at the station."

"You could come with me down this track and see where we end up." Krista's tone might be light, but her expression was dead serious. "According to Desz, we have chemistry and a comfortable interview style that the camera loves."

The thought of working with Krista was tempting. Incredibly tempting. He shook his head. "You were born to be in front of cameras. Me, not so much. I'm an athlete, not a performer."

"Models are meant to be seen, not heard. I bet with all your post-game interviews, you've spent more time actually speaking in front of a camera than I have." Krista reached over and intertwined her fingers with his. "Besides, the more I think about it, I'm not sure it really even matters. What we've done in the past doesn't have to define what we do in the future. There's no reason we can't search for options outside our box. Doing so opens up many more possibilities."

"Maybe," he said, then nodded. "Probably."

"I'm betting that when you've looked ahead to life after hockey, you've only been considering positions within the box."

"That's where my experience lies," Dustin reminded her, then took a pull of beer. "I hear what you're saying, and I don't disagree. I believe you can do anything. But for me, the time and energy and resources I've invested in my career—invested in myself—mean a lot. And I'm good at what I do. There's a logic to doing what we're good at. Isn't that why you started your search by making a list? Soar with your strengths and all that?"

"Soaring with your strengths doesn't mean staying in a box." Krista met his gaze. "Not for me. Or you."

CHAPTER FIFTEEN

Krista couldn't have predicted that seeing Kevin in that ugly sweater during the Catwalk event would spur another *Holly*wood Stars event. Maybe it was true that being creative fostered even more creativity.

When she and Dustin met with Kenny the day after the Catwalk, she happened to say how fun it would be to have an Ugly Sweater Parade. When Dustin chimed in that they should bring in a marching band, Kenny mentioned adding decorated lawn tractors. The idea had quickly taken on a life of its own.

Now, three days later, visitors were flooding downtown Holly Pointe on Saturday morning for another Holly Days event.

Dozens of lawn tractors, driven by people wearing ugly sweaters, chugged down Main Street. Entrants had gone all out decorating their vehicles. Krista spotted a lighted reindeer perched on the top of one tractor and a real tree in the back of another's trailer, fully decorated with music pulsing in time to the flashing lights.

Striding down the street in front of Sam's tractor, Kevin and fellow supporters of the local animal shelter wore the most gawdawful sweaters while walking dogs in Pawsibility sweaters. Lulu, thankfully, was nowhere in sight.

Lucy, dressed as Santa's helper, drove her own decorated tractor and tossed beads to kids along the route.

Spectators lined both curbs as the parade slowly made its way down the street. Teenagers wearing Santa hats and the requisite ugly sweater tossed candy to onlookers.

Children scrambled from their perches on the curbs to scoop up the colorfully wrapped pieces.

Wearing attire purchased for last year's holiday competition, members of the Holly Pointe High School band wore sweaters that sported sayings like "O Come All Ye Flute-ful" and "O Drum All Ye Faithful."

"'We Wish You a Merry Christmas' sounds different coming from a marching band," Krista told Dustin as they walked the route side by side, waving and smiling. "I can't believe all the people."

Dustin grinned. "Kenny told me this morning they were anticipating the largest single-day crowd they've ever had for Holly Days."

"Probably because of today's parade and the pond hockey game this afternoon."

Dustin nodded. "We had twice as many kids show up to the hockey clinic this morning compared to yesterday's."

"How's that going?"

"Good." Dustin smiled. "They're eager and excited to learn."

"According to Desz, a whole crowd of kids and their parents swarmed Rosie's Diner this morning after your hockey clinic."

"Speaking of Desz, where is she?" Dustin asked, as if just now noticing her absence.

"Waitressing at Rosie's." Krista smiled. "A couple of waitresses called in sick. When Desz heard that they were short a server, she offered to fill in."

"She's a good person."

"She is," Krista agreed. "Do you know she already sent an email to her Aunt Sondra and Uncle Percy, asking them to contact me?"

"No grass growing under her feet, or yours."

Krista glanced down at her snow boots, then back up at him. "Not a single blade."

"I'm excited for you." They continued down the street, smiling and waving to the crowd. "Me, I feel as if I'm in a holding pattern. I don't much like it."

Surprise skittered through her. "I thought you'd decided you weren't going back if you weren't a hundred percent."

Dustin blew out a breath. "That's how I feel, but I still can't let go. I realize that doesn't make sense. When I think about walking away from hockey, this little voice inside my head keeps reminding me that not everyone on the team plays at the same level, gives the same effort. Could I play at a lesser level and still feel good about myself?"

"That's something only you can answer." Krista kept her voice matter-of-fact. "What about your knee? Are you willing to risk damaging it irreparably simply for another couple years of playing?"

"Those are hard-hitting questions." His lips quirked in a humorless smile. "Ones I don't have an answer to right now."

"If you haven't made a firm decision that you're going back, why not consider other options?"

"Another good question." He shoved his hands into his pockets. "I can see myself as maybe being a broadcaster, but that's down the line. Right now, I just can't get my brain to think about anything but hockey."

Krista's heart went out to him. Over the years her love affair with modeling had cooled, but there had been a time when she couldn't imagine not doing it. "Have you spoken with your agent?"

"Not yet." He slanted a quick glance in her direction. "What about you? Does Merline know what you're planning?"

"No." Krista shook her head for extra emphasis. "I prefer to discuss future plans with her face-to-face and only once I'm sure of my plans. Hopefully, I'll hear from Desz's relatives soon."

A wolf whistle split the air.

"Hey, Krista," a man called. "Will you marry me?"

She only shook her head and laughed.

Dustin grabbed her hand and gave it a swing.

"The offer to join me in this venture has no expiration date." She offered him a bright smile. "We'd make a great team."

"Of that," Dustin agreed, "I have no doubt."

By the time they returned to their cabins, Dustin's mind was still racing. The last thing he wanted to do was spend the last few hours before the pond hockey game contemplating his future. The trouble was, he couldn't seem to shut off the thoughts.

As if sensing his stress, Krista tugged him to a stop in front of his cabin. "You've been awfully quiet."

Gazing into her cobalt-blue eyes, Dustin answered honestly. "I can't stop thinking about my future."

"There's no reason you have to make a decision right now, is there?"

"No, but that doesn't stop me from considering options." He gave a little laugh. "It's like my mind is on this revolving loop that I can't shut off."

"Invite me inside." Krista leaned up and kissed him along his jaw. "I believe I can get your mind focused on something else."

Dustin made quick work of unlocking the door. Once inside, he pulled Krista into his arms and kissed her.

"You figured out how I planned to distract that busy mind of yours." Humor danced in her eyes as her arms slipped around his neck.

"Let's just say I hoped." Dustin closed his mouth over hers and gave in to the feel and taste of her.

As they continued to kiss, her fingers sliding into his hair and her mouth opening to the sweep of his tongue, thoughts of his messed-up career and the decisions that needed to be made drifted away. The endless loop in his head finally quieted.

Giving in to the emotion rising inside him, Dustin found himself determined to show Krista by every touch, every caress, every kiss how much she meant to him. The depth of his feelings shocked and thrilled. He'd never felt this way about any woman before.

Dustin wasn't sure how this would end, but one thing he knew—Krista was not only the one woman he couldn't get enough of, she was the woman he loved.

CHAPTER SIXTEEN

The area around the pond that afternoon had a circus atmosphere. Brilliant lights illuminated the pond and its banks. Vendors offered those watching the game a wide variety of food and drinks. Santa had arrived, perched on the seat of a horse-drawn wagon, the black horses sporting bells and colorfully braided manes.

Next to Santa sat Mrs. Claus, making Krista wonder who was watching the Busy Bean.

Children surrounded the wagon when it stopped, while parents stood back, snapping pictures that would find their way into their social media.

Krista and Desz had planned to arrive early, but the steady stream of traffic headed toward the pond had the trip taking twice as long.

"Look." Desz pointed. "That's the ABC affiliate out of Burlington. I saw more vans from other stations in the parking lot."

Krista didn't even ask if Desz was sure. If anyone knew communications of all types, it was her friend.

"Why would a television station be here?"

Desz shot her a disbelieving glance. "Because of Dustin."

"This is a pond hockey game," Krista reminded her friend.

"It's the first appearance on ice of a Stanley Cup MVP since his injury."

A lump formed in Krista's stomach. She hoped Dustin would be able to see this game for what it was—a fun time on the ice to raise awareness for Holly Days.

Krista lifted her chin. She had complete confidence in Dustin's ability to put on a good show. And if any of the media eyes turned her way, they would see only what she wanted them to see—not a speck of worry from his fellow *Holly*wood Star, only pride and enthusiasm.

Instead of her parka, she wore her cashmere coat, the one that flattered her lithe figure. She knotted a cobalt-blue plaid scarf carelessly around her neck.

Her leggings were tucked into boots that managed to be attractive despite their rubber soles. Instead of the mittens with glove liners she'd donned in recent days, she wore leather gloves that made her hands appear long and slender.

She'd taken extra care with her makeup this morning and knew she looked her best. It was all part of the image and a persona she was comfortable inhabiting.

As the pond came into sight, Krista searched for Dustin. She found him with a group of men, all wearing red jerseys. On the other side of the frozen ice, another group of men, wearing blue, gathered.

Someone—Kenny or the town council—had had benches set up for the onlookers. It was clear to Krista that there was no chance that she and Desz—along with most of the others in the crowd—would get a seat.

"We should look for a place to stand," she told Desz. "One that will give us a good—"

"Mrs. Santa is waving us over." Desz pointed to where Norma stood in her Mrs. Santa garb near the ice.

For a second, Krista wondered if Desz could be mistaken.

After all, there could be a lot of people Norma might be waving to right now. But when she glanced her way and made eye contact with the woman, Krista realized Desz was right.

Only when she drew close did Krista realize that Norma was waving her to where the news media congregated.

"Show time," Krista said under her breath to Desz.

"Once we get close," Desz said in the same low tone, "I'll step back."

"No, you don't—"

"It's you and Dustin they want." Desz's voice was firm and brooked no argument. "You're the *Holly*wood Stars."

Krista really couldn't argue with that. Besides, they were nearly there.

Santa had plucked Dustin out of the team, and he now stood there, waiting.

She'd wondered if he had some kind of pregame ritual they were interrupting, but if he did, he didn't appear disturbed by being forced to interact with the media.

"There she is." Santa spoke in a hearty tone befitting his red suit. "Our second *Holly*wood Star, the always lovely Krista Ankrom."

A tall man with piercing brown eyes smiled at Krista. "Would you move closer to Mr. Bellamy? I'd like some shots of the two of you together."

Krista smiled and moved to Dustin's side.

The welcome in his eyes warmed her. Because she knew him so well, Krista knew he'd likely been dreading this part of today, when he'd face reporters who'd undoubtedly come to dredge up his injury and talk about his future.

Well, she was here to make sure that didn't happen.

"You two have been spending a lot of time together since coming to Holly Pointe." A male reporter sporting black-rimmed glasses shifted his sharp-eyed gaze between her and Dustin. "Do you plan to pursue your friendship once the holidays are over?"

Krista understood some reporters had a certain narrative in mind, but now that she had real feelings for Dustin, the questions seemed like an invasion of privacy. Then she reminded herself that talk of romance would keep the questions off hockey.

Shifting slightly to offer the cameras her best angle, Krista smiled. "I don't believe either of us is ready for this holiday to end."

Shutters clicked.

"How does it feel to be spending time with one of the most beautiful women in the world?" the man with the dark-rimmed glasses asked Dustin.

Extravagant praise, but again, it was all about image.

"The thing that most people don't realize, and I didn't discover until we reunited in Holly Pointe, is that Krista is as beautiful on the inside as out." Dustin pushed back a tendril of her hair with one finger, his gaze firmly focused on her. "Spending time with her has been amazing."

"Reunited?" The female reporter's gaze sharpened. "You knew each other before?"

Obviously, Krista thought, someone hadn't done her research.

"Dustin and I came here every Christmas growing up." She smiled. "Our families' cabins were right next door to each other."

"Do you remember him from back then?" the female reporter asked.

"What do you think?" Krista cast a flirty glance in Dustin's direction. "This guy is impossible to forget."

"When do you think you'll be returning—" a man began.

Santa lifted a hand. "I apologize for cutting this short, but Dustin has a game to play."

Acting on impulse, Krista leaned over and brushed a kiss across Dustin's cheek. "Good luck."

"Thanks." Dustin gave her hand a squeeze before hitting the ice and skating off.

"The best place for you to view the match is right over here."

Norma pointed, then motioned for the press to follow her. "Let's hurry so you don't miss a thing."

"Thanks, Santa," Krista said to Kenny.

"You two played that perfectly." Kenny gave an approving nod. "Anyone watching the two of you would think you're falling in love."

"I think Holly Days will get some good press." *Falling in love.* Seeing Dustin today, feeling the overwhelming urge to protect him from reporters hounding him about his future in hockey, had Krista accepting what she'd already known. She wasn't just *on the verge* of falling in love with Dustin.

She'd already fallen.

She only wished she knew if he felt the same.

Dustin blocked out all thoughts of Krista as he took the ice with his teammates. They'd put on quite a show for the reporters, which should guarantee plenty of free publicity for Holly Days. Now that that task was done, the focus needed to be on the game.

Just being on the ice again was a heady experience and had him wondering if he should try to go back to his team in January.

First things first, he told himself. He was too much of a competitor not to give this game his full effort.

When he'd first arrived, Sam had asked if he planned to give it his all. Dustin had told him honestly that he didn't know any other way to play.

Besides, he knew his Holly Pointe teammates were counting on him, and the guys on the other team, composed of players from surrounding areas, were gunning for him.

Dustin smiled. Let the fun begin.

It wasn't even close.

The crazy thing was no one seemed to care. Oh, all the other players gave their top effort, but having him on the Holly Pointe team was too powerful of a weapon.

Ten. Nine. Eight.

The crowd counted down the seconds until the game ended. It had been a festive atmosphere from the start with loud cheers and boos throughout the game.

Six. Five. Four.

Dustin had the puck and took his time crossing the ice. His team had already scored so many points, there was no need to score another.

Still, his fight-to-the-finish mentality had him watching the goalie.

Was the guy really counting down with the crowd? Hadn't he been taught that the game wasn't over until the buzzer sounded?

"Two."

With one swift movement, Dustin shot the puck to the goalie's left. It went in.

"One."

Then the game was over, and everyone was cheering.

Dustin accepted the pats on the back and the congratulations even as his gaze searched the crowd for Krista. She remained where she'd been seated since the game began, near Desz, Kenny and Norma.

He didn't go to her, but stayed with the team as they shook hands with the opposing players.

"Great game." The guy from the opposing team was familiar.

Only after he'd skated away did Dustin place him. He was a relative of Dustin's coach. Not a son, but a nephew or something who'd shown up a couple of times to watch practice.

The team planned to gather at a local tavern to celebrate. Dustin told them he'd try to stop by.

He liked the guys on the team, but other than Kevin and Sam, he didn't know them all that well.

He started over toward Krista, but changed course when his phone buzzed with a text from her.

Media is relentless! Save yourself. I've got this.

He took one more glance in her direction and saw her laughing and joking with the press, and that told him she really did have it under control. Or she was giving a darn good imitation.

After gathering his gear, he fell into step with other team members, then veered off when he thought no one was watching. Sam had shown him a secluded spot to park down the road so that he wouldn't be stuck in the lot where everyone else parked.

Dustin was nearly there when he heard someone call his name. He whirled.

Not the female reporter, as he'd feared, but Desz, huffing and puffing.

"Don't you know how to saunter?" she asked, pausing to catch her breath.

"I guess I must have skipped school the day that was taught."

He liked Desz. Liked that she was a good friend to Krista. Liked that even though she made her living blogging, he didn't need to worry about her blogging about him.

"Are you looking for Krista?" he asked. "Because I'm pretty sure she's still charming the press."

"I was looking for you."

He slowed his steps. "What can I do for you?"

"For starters, you can give me a ride."

"Sure," he agreed. "Where do you want to go?"

"Would you mind taking me out to Kevin's place? He's having a few friends over. You and I are invited." When he hesitated, she smiled. "Krista will meet us there."

Dustin smiled.

"I thought that would change your mind." Desz smug tone had his smile widening.

They reached the SUV, and Dustin opened the passenger door

for Desz. "Neither Kevin nor Sam mentioned getting together after the game."

"They didn't want to alert the other players, who might alert the media." Desz waited until Dustin was behind the wheel before continuing. "Besides, downtown is sure to be crazy busy and crawling with reporters. How did it feel to be back on the ice?"

"Great. I had fun."

"I'd love to interview you sometime for my blog." Desz tossed out the words. "The focus would be on how finding our passion leads to a fulfilling life and career. I wouldn't ask questions about your injury or future plans. You have my word on that."

He slanted her a sideways glance and pulled out onto the road. "How's your blog going?"

Her lips curved as she pointed a nail as red as her lips at him.

"I'm on to you. You don't want to talk about yourself, so you're shifting the focus to me." She flashed a smile. "Good thing I like talking about myself."

He laughed, understanding why she and Krista were such good friends.

"The blog is doing quite well, thank you very much." Satisfaction filled Desz's dark eyes. "When I started it several years back, I struggled to find my audience. That's no problem now."

"Do you think you'll keep doing it?"

"I'm not sure."

"That surprises me. It sounds as if you love it, and you're good at it." He made another turn, glancing in the rearview to make sure no one was following them.

"I do love it." Desz airily gestured with one hand. "But I'm in a constantly evolving industry where, to survive and thrive, I need to be able to pivot."

Dustin nodded, keeping his focus on the road. "Everything changes."

"It certainly does." Desz let out a happy sigh. "That's what makes life exciting."

CHAPTER SEVENTEEN

It took Krista longer than she'd anticipated to extricate herself from the media. The reporters appeared reluctant to leave, no doubt hoping to snag face time with Dustin after the game.

When someone mentioned the team had left for the Thirsty Moose for a postgame celebration, the reporters made a beeline for their cars.

Krista smiled as she sauntered to her own car, enjoying the feel of cool, crisp air against her face while she inhaled the fresh scent of pine.

Though she loved urban living, she was coming to realize just how much she enjoyed the freedom that came from not always being surrounded by people.

The parking lot was nearly deserted, and she hoped all those people who'd been parked here had either headed to the Market-place or into Holly Pointe.

The Mistletoe Ball was next on the schedule, unless she and Dustin managed to think of another *Holly*wood Stars event in the final week leading up to Christmas.

Krista smiled. She wouldn't put it past her and Dustin to

come up with another activity. Over the past two weeks, they'd become creative in all sorts of ways.

Krista's phone buzzed, notifying her she had a text from Desz. *D and I will see you at Kevin's.*

On my way, Krista texted back, glad Desz had been able to catch a ride with Dustin.

The thumbs-up Desz sent had Krista smiling as she slid behind the driver's seat. Desz was another blessing to come from this trip. They'd been friends for several years, but Krista felt as if she understood Desz so much better now.

Before this trip, she'd viewed Desz as almost too goal-oriented. Now, she saw that her friend had fought hard to build her name in a difficult arena and wasn't about to lose out by taking her eyes off the ball.

Focusing on her own future might be front and center in Krista's mind, but tonight she planned to relax and enjoy. Tuning the radio to a station playing "all Christmas songs, all the time," she smiled at the upbeat song about Grandma and a reckless reindeer.

The smile faded as a romantic Christmas ballad filled the air next. This trip, even her position as a *Holly*wood Star, had been especially wonderful because of Dustin.

Reuniting with him had been a joy. The problem with reunions was they were too often temporary. She would soon go back to her world, and he'd go back to his.

She told herself they could make a long-distance romance work, but she'd been in a short one early in her career and knew the challenges.

She switched the station to something fun and upbeat.

The rest of the drive went quickly, and anticipation surged when she recognized the vehicles parked in the drive at Kevin's. She pulled in behind Dustin's Jeep.

The door opened when she reached the steps. Lucy greeted her with a warm smile and a hug. "I'm so glad you could make it."

"Thanks for inviting me." Krista glanced around. She'd expected—hoped—to see Dustin once she stepped inside. "Where is everyone?"

Lucy laughed. "Sam is showing Kevin and Dustin a new game he picked up that he wants us all to play."

"Did she tell you what the game is?" Desz strolled out of the kitchen, pausing to take a sip from the cup she held. "I asked, but Lucy wouldn't tell me."

Krista glanced curiously at Lucy.

"I can't." Lucy shook her head, regret blanketing her face. "Sam and Kevin want to surprise you both."

"But they're showing Dustin," Desz pointed out.

Lucy lifted her hands, let them drop.

"You and Kevin sure do love Christmas." Desz glanced around the living room, signs of holiday cheer everywhere.

"I never cared much about the holidays," Lucy admitted, "until Kevin and I got together."

Krista sensed a story here. "What changed?"

"Let me get you a cup of hot apple cider first." Lucy disappeared into the kitchen, returning less than a minute later. She handed Krista the steaming cup.

"It's quite good," Desz said in response to Krista's questioning look.

Taking a sip, Krista smiled. "I like it."

"You asked what changed. I'm an only child." Lucy's fingers curved around a bright red mug with a Santa face. "While I was growing up, my mother was more into her boyfriends and husbands than celebrating the holidays with me."

"Husbands?" Desz asked.

"She's had four." Lucy spoke matter-of-factly, as if relaying an updated weather report. "She's got a new guy, but he won't last."

Krista thought of her own, very stable, childhood. "I'm sorry."

"It is what it is." Lucy shrugged. "Having her take trips with her latest guy over the holidays was pretty much a given."

"What did you do?" Krista sipped the cider.

"Stayed with relatives. Or friends." A tiny smile lifted Lucy's lips. "Once Kevin and I started dating, I began spending holidays with him and his family."

"I didn't realize you and Kevin had been together that long." Desz's tone reflected her astonishment.

"We started dating when we were fifteen." Lucy's eyes took on a distant glow. "We've been together seven years."

Desz cocked her head. "Were you apart during college?"

"We both went to UVM." Lucy sat back, cradling her cup with both hands. "Kevin could have gone anywhere, but he wanted to be with me. I had to go to a state school. My mom wasn't about to pony up out-of-state tuition."

"I'm surprised you didn't get married once you graduated." Krista couldn't believe she'd voiced the thought. Clearly, her Midwestern roots were showing.

Lucy shrugged. "I love Kevin. I know he loves me. But I'm in no hurry to get married. Kevin is willing to wait until I am."

"You want to wait because of your mom." Desz put out the statement and let it lie.

"Probably." Lucy picked at a string on the cotton throw tossed over the arm of the sofa. "When you've seen as many men come and go as I have, you know promises of forever mean nothing. Even when you know you have the right man, it's difficult to think of walking down that aisle. And really, what is marriage but a piece of paper?"

Krista didn't argue with her point. She knew plenty of successful men and women who vowed to never marry, who considered the institution to be the first step toward ruining a perfectly good relationship.

"What about you?" Lucy fixed warm blue eyes on Krista.

"I've been too busy with my career to even date much," Krista admitted. "I've never found anyone who made me think of forever."

Until Dustin, she added silently.

"I'm still building my career," Desz asserted when Lucy's questioning gaze settled on her.

Krista decided it was time to change the subject. She didn't want to think how she'd found the right man and how she might have to let him go. "You do an amazing job managing the activities at the barns."

"My mom got enough out of divorce number four to build them." Lucy's chuckle held little humor. "She's really good at event planning when she sets her mind to it. Unfortunately, the novelty quickly wore off. Grace Hollow was really struggling when I took over the management."

"How's it doing now?" Desz asked.

"In the black." Lucy perked up at the sound of the back door being pushed open. She was on her feet when Kevin, followed by Dustin and Sam, strode into the room.

Kevin moved immediately to Lucy and gave her a quick kiss. "Sorry that took so long."

Sam held up his hands. "Blame it on me."

"Not your fault," Kevin insisted. "The game took longer to set up. Then we pestered Dustin to show us some hockey moves."

"We're going to have so much fun." Lucy leaned her head back as Kevin draped an arm around her shoulders and kissed her again lightly.

Dustin moved to sit on the arm of Krista's chair. "I hated leaving you to fight off the wolves by yourself."

"They were very kind wolves. To me." Krista felt herself settle. It was as if all was right in her world now that he was beside her. "They took off running when they heard the team was gathering for a postgame celebration at the Thirsty Moose."

Dustin shifted his gaze to Sam and Kevin. "Another reason to thank you for tonight's invitation."

"What game is it we're playing?" Krista asked Dustin in a low tone.

Dustin leaned close to Krista's ear, his mouth only an inch away when he whispered, "Bowling."

Krista gazed at him quizzically, knowing she must have misheard.

"No telling secrets." Desz spoke loudly as she pointed at Dustin and Krista. "Unless you're telling them to me."

"Any excuse to get close," Lucy said with a knowing glance.

There was no arguing with that, at least not in Krista's mind. She wanted Dustin close, as close as he'd been the nights that they'd made love.

Her breath quickened at the thought. As she looked up and met Dustin's gaze, the devilish gleam in his eyes made her realize there were no secrets. Not between them.

They were definitely on the same page.

Dustin's bowling experiences during college had always involved beer and betting.

This activity, set up in Kevin and Sam's backyard, involved a lane made out of snow and competition with men and women intent on winning.

"I can't believe we're using real bowling pins," Dustin murmured as he watched Sam set up a pin that had fallen over.

For this first game, Kevin had volunteered to be the pinsetter, but Sam assured them they would each get the opportunity.

Opportunity didn't seem the right word to Dustin, but he didn't call him on it, not when Sam was so excited to show Desz and Krista the game now that it was all set up.

"We'll use a regular bowling ball to knock down the pins," Dustin told Krista.

"You each get two throws." Sam's serious gaze scanned the group. "Lucy will record your score, then we'll move on to the next. Once everyone has tossed, then whoever knocked down the most pins that round wins."

"What happens if there's a tie?"

Dustin wasn't surprised the question came from Krista. The woman had a mind for details.

"Then we have a bowl-off to determine the winner," Sam advised.

"Ladies first." Lucy gestured to Desz and Krista.

The two women exchanged glances. Finally, Desz shrugged. "I'll give it a go."

It was obvious to Dustin by the way Desz held the ball that she'd bowled before, though she knocked over only three pins on her first throw and two on her next.

Dustin chose to go last, preferring to analyze the others' techniques and the way the icy-smooth lane of ice pulled. It reminded him of watching game films, looking for an opponent's weakness.

The lane consistently pulled to the left. From observing Sam, Dustin learned that the correct throwing position, as well as a forceful throw, was essential to knocking down the maximum number of pins.

Even as Dustin told himself this was just a game with the purpose of having fun, he moved his starting position from the center of the alley to the far right.

Gliding to the "line" in the snow, but stopping just short, Dustin released the ball. With narrowed eyes, he watched it pull to the left as expected.

A smile blossomed on his lips. There was nothing better than when careful observation paid off.

The loud clatter that sounded when his ball hit the pins, knocking them into each other, was music to his ears.

"Steeee-*rike*," Kevin called out, pumping a fist in the air. "Dustin wins this round."

Krista flung her arms around his neck and kissed him. "Congratulations."

He liked the feel of her against him, liked it a little too much when they were surrounded by people. Conscious of everyone watching, he tugged a piece of Krista's hair. "Next time, it's your turn."

Next time, it was her turn *to win*. Apparently, he wasn't the only one who could read the alley.

By the time they finished their game and put away the pins and ball, the wind had picked up.

"Let's go inside." Lucy wrapped her arms around herself to ward off the chill. "I'll get the fondue going."

"This has been fun." Krista exchanged a smile with Desz. "I never knew snow-bowling existed."

"I didn't either," Desz admitted. "But I got some good shots of the lanes and pins, and this is going in my blog."

"If you want," Sam told Desz, "I'd be happy to give you the history of the sport."

Krista moved even closer to Dustin and lowered her voice. "I did better once I figured out the lane pulled to the left."

"It's crazy how you and I are always on the same wavelength."

She tapped her temple with a bent index finger. "Great minds."

Dustin laughed and slung an arm around her shoulders, realizing how right it felt. He kept his voice soft, for her ears only. "Will you watch a movie with me later?"

Krista gazed up at him through lowered lashes. "Is that all you can offer?"

"Microwave popcorn?"

"I was thinking more about…" She paused as if conscious of the others several feet away. "You know… More."

A slow smile lifted his lips. "Definitely more."

Krista returned his smile. "Count me in."

CHAPTER EIGHTEEN

Krista slanted Desz a sideways glance as she pointed the Subaru toward home. While the fondue selections had been excellent and the conversation relaxed and easy, she'd been ready to leave when Desz had mentioned she had an early-morning interview.

Desz slipped her iPad from her purse as soon as she buckled in. As if she sensed Krista staring, she looked up and smiled. "My blog traffic has exploded since I came to Holly Pointe."

"It doesn't seem like you're getting much R&R while you're here."

"I don't mind. I love the blog." Desz's lips curved. "And I enjoy doing everything associated with it. Responding to comments, checking stats, writing and uploading new posts. It doesn't feel like work."

"Modeling was like that at first for me." Krista vividly recalled those early days. "It was stressful, sure, but so very exciting. I remember how thrilled I was when I got my first international shoot. My family did a lot of traveling when I was growing up, but always in the United States. When I stepped onto that flight to Milan, I had goose bumps." She gave a little laugh. "You've done a lot of European travel, but for me—"

"It was a milestone. A big one." Desz smiled. "I experienced that same thrill when my blog got featured on that Buzzfeed list of bloggers to watch."

"That was definitely an awesome moment." Krista clasped her hands in her lap. "I'm excited for this next stage in my life. But I'm also scared."

Desz arched a brow.

"I'm worried it might not work out." Krista took a breath, then let it out. "Then there's Dustin. You probably think I'm foolish to have gotten involved with him when I'm supposed to be making plans and taking control of my future."

When Desz took a second to respond, Krista braced herself.

"I don't think you're foolish." Desz offered an encouraging smile. "You'll never know whether this new direction works or your relationship with Dustin is strong enough to go the distance if you don't try."

"I like him, Desz. A lot. In fact, I love him." Saying the words aloud hadn't been nearly as difficult as Krista had imagined. Maybe because she trusted Desz implicitly.

"That isn't a surprise." Desz smiled. "I've seen how you look at him. And how he looks at you."

"Do you think anyone else noticed?" Krista's voice rose. While she wasn't ashamed of her feelings for Dustin, her love for him was shiny and new, and she wanted to keep it close, at least for now.

"Probably." Desz's lips quirked upward. "Though even if you weren't in love with him, people see what they want to see. And what they want to see is their *Holly*wood Stars in love. If you were in their place, isn't that what you'd want?"

Krista gave a reluctant nod.

"I know you're concerned about the future. But just like modeling, if Dustin ends up not being forever, you'll be okay. The love you're sharing with him won't be any less meaningful." Desz reached over and gave Krista's arm a comforting squeeze. "Don't let fear of failure stop you from trying, in life or in love."

Krista gave a jerky nod. "Dustin invited me over to his cabin tonight."

"Which works out wonderfully, as I'm ready to begin writing a post on my snow-bowling experience."

While Desz headed to her room with her laptop, Krista headed next door.

The door to Dustin's cabin opened after her first knock.

His eyes darkened with pleasure at the sight of her. "Welcome."

As soon as she stepped inside, Dustin pulled her to him and held on. "I've been waiting to do this all day."

Relaxing against him, Krista expelled a contented sigh. "Me, too." After a long minute, she stepped back and met his gaze. "I'm glad you invited me."

His gaze traveled slowly over her. "I'm glad you accepted."

They stood there for several heartbeats, grinning at each other like two fools, or two people madly in love.

Dustin broke the silence first. "What can I get you to drink?"

"Wine?"

"Can do." He gestured to the sofa. "Have a seat, and I'll bring it to you."

Instead of sitting, she followed him into the kitchen and leaned against the doorjamb. She studied him while he retrieved the wine, pouring two glasses of red.

He moved with the grace of an athlete. That's how he saw himself, but that wasn't all he was, any more than she was simply a model. They were people first, with needs and desires and dreams.

"You looked good on the ice today." Accepting the glass he offered, she took a sip.

"The guys didn't—" He stopped himself before he could say more and appeared to change tacks. "They weren't experienced, so it was easy to look good."

"Any twinges or pain?"

He followed her into the living room, the palm of his free hand resting against her back. "No, but I wasn't forced to put any pressure on the knee joint."

Krista lifted a brow. "No dekes?"

He laughed and shook his head. When she dropped down on the sofa, he sat beside her.

"Well, I'm glad it went well." Krista leaned back against the arm he slipped around her shoulders. "By the time the reporters took off in search of you, Mr. NHL," Krista gestured with her wineglass to Dustin, "the parking lot was empty. Hopefully, that meant everyone was either shopping at the Marketplace or downtown."

"I feel good we were able to do our part." Dustin's gaze met hers. "I owe you for diverting those reporters."

"Seriously, it was no biggie." Waving an airy hand, Krista sipped her wine. "You'd have done the same for me."

"Definitely." His beautiful gray eyes went dove-soft as they searched hers. "What are we going to do, Krista?"

Something about the serious tone of his voice sent her pulse skittering. "About?"

"About us."

Dustin had always prided himself on knowing where he was headed, but right now he felt as if he were walking on shifting sand in a direction he hadn't plotted out.

"I can't walk away from you." He reached over and took her

hand, relieved when her fingers curved around his. "I don't want what we're building to end."

"I don't want that either."

Her comment had him expelling the breath he hadn't realized he'd been holding. While he might not have all the answers, he was an expert at making things happen.

"I spoke with my agent right before you got here," he murmured, twining the strands of her hair loosely around his fingers.

"Freddie finally wore you down with the endless calls and texts."

"I decided to give the poor guy a break and answer his call." Dustin's tone had been as lighthearted as hers, then it turned serious. "He gave me some straight talk when I told him I hadn't ruled out going back to the team."

Her brow furrowed as she processed his words. "Not to be negative, but if you do that, and it doesn't work out, could they move you to another team? Or to the minors?"

Dustin shook his head. "I have a full no-move clause. If I try and fail, then I'm done."

"What kind of straight talk did he give you?"

"He reminded me that I won't be at my full level going back, and that means, frankly, less money. Certainly, I have my contract, but Freddie thinks I'll lose endorsements and other opportunities—like coaching or broadcasting—because I won't be coming at them as an MVP, but as a fading star."

She studied him over the rim of her glass.

"Freddie mentioned a possible coaching opportunity." Dustin told himself he was lucky to have an agent who presented all options. "The position is at a university known for producing players that go on to the NHL."

"Sounds right up your alley." Krista's tone gave him no indica-tion how she was feeling. "Coaching makes sense, considering your years in the sport."

"I suppose it does." Dustin had told Freddie to get more information on the position, but oddly, he had been unable to summon much enthusiasm.

"But it won't be the same as playing."

"No."

Krista's tremulous smile didn't quite reach her eyes. "It's good to have options."

"Going back and failing isn't what I want. At this point, if I tell them I'm not coming back, then I'll be going out on top. Coaching… Well, I'm not sure it's what I want." Dustin expelled a breath. "It's an easy option because it's within the box."

Their conversation the other night had stuck with him, had actually nagged at him, he admitted.

"It is, and I stand by what I said about being open to options outside the box. But just because it's in your wheelhouse or your box doesn't make it *automatically* a wrong choice either," she pointed out.

"Are you still looking to pursue the television show?" he asked abruptly.

"I am," she admitted. "Or rather, I'm exploring that option. I'm hoping to meet with Desz's relatives in January, see what information they can give me."

"I assume you'll do research on competing shows, stuff like that?"

"Yes, and there will likely be some start-up costs and a business plan, of which I know nothing about." She gave a little laugh. "But I'm an intelligent woman. I'll learn whatever I need to know in order to make a good decision."

"I was a business major in college." Dustin met her gaze. "I know all about business plans."

"Does that mean I can count on you as a resource?"

"Absolutely. If you're still interested, I'd also like to explore the option of this being something we do together."

Krista's frowned in puzzlement. "I don't understand why

you're suddenly interested. I mean, I'm happy you are, but the other night, you said you weren't ready to think about it. Now you've got these other opportunities, so what's going on?"

"Honestly, I'm not sure." Dustin lifted his hands, then let them drop. "I'm not sure exactly what I should do, and that uncertainty makes me feel lost." He met her questioning gaze. "Then I think about you, and I feel found. You make me feel like myself, like I can figure things out. I haven't felt that way since my injury."

The soft look that filled her eyes prompted him to continue. "I've thought a lot about our earlier conversation and the tough questions you asked." Dustin pulled his brows together. "I don't want to screw up my ACL so bad that I can't even enjoy a game of pond hockey. And I've never been a guy who can give whatever I do less than a hundred and ten percent. So, even if I went back and risked everything, I don't think it would work."

"You have given this more thought."

Dustin flashed a smile. "Besides, you and me, we make a stellar team."

She smiled back. "You're good at staying focused and planning."

"You're creative. Even more, when I'm with you, I feel comfortable in the spotlight." Dustin wrapped his arms around her, pulling her close. "I don't want to let go of what we have, Krista. I don't want to lose you."

When her arms slid around his neck and their mouths met, Dustin knew he was right where he belonged and with the one he was meant to be with.

The last week leading up to the Mistletoe Ball on Friday had been filled with one final Selfie with the Stars appearance and a Dustin-led hockey clinic for anyone eighteen and over.

Dustin told Krista that as much as he enjoyed the clinic, it only solidified his belief that full-time coaching wasn't for him.

Desz's uncle had gotten in touch, and Krista was relieved at how excited Percy seemed about her concept.

By Thursday, excitement quivered in the pit of Krista's stomach. While a business plan still needed to be developed, the possible had become probable.

They were going to do this, Krista thought, both excited and terrified by the prospect.

Krista had brought a dress with her from New York for the Mistletoe Ball. But when she'd been at One More Time choosing her dress for the Catwalk, a red velvet Worth evening gown with a jeweled lace collar had caught her eye.

Not only would she feel like a princess in the red velvet, renting the lovely gown from One More Time would give her the opportunity to promote the small business one last time.

Desz's indrawn breath had her whirling.

"You look amazing." Desz stared at the lace interspersed with pearls. "A real *Holly*wood Star."

"You want to know the best part?"

"You'll be there with Dustin."

"Well, yes, that, too." Krista smiled. "I won't be walking the red carpet while holding on to a pig."

"You loved hanging out with Lulu. You know you did," Desz teased.

"She's a sweetheart," Krista reluctantly admitted. "But one time with her was definitely enough."

"Enough about pigs. Come into the bedroom." Desz grabbed Krista's hand and tugged. "There's a full-length mirror on the back of the door. You have to get the total effect."

In the past, Krista had donned evening wear that cost tens of thousands of dollars. She'd had her hair and makeup done by experts in the field. But gazing at herself now in the yellowed mirror, never had she felt more beautiful.

Even her hair, hanging in loose curls to her shoulders, seemed to possess extra shine.

"Where are your shoes?" Desz demanded.

Krista only continued to stare at herself in the mirror. A smile slowly curved her lips as she imagined Dustin's reaction when he saw her.

How lovely it was going to be to dance with him. She couldn't wait to hold him close under the mistletoe ball in the beautiful barn at Grace Hollow.

"Krista."

Desz's voice broke through her fanciful thoughts. "Shoes. Show me your shoes."

Krista waved a hand in the direction of the closet. "My sparkly pumps are in there."

Seconds later, she sat on the bed to put on the shoes Desz had brought her, then stood and twirled.

"Yes." Desz nodded approvingly. "Very nice."

"You need to try on your dress," Krista told her. "I haven't seen it on you."

"It fits," Desz told her. "I tried it on earlier."

"I didn't see it." Krista turned. "Unfasten me, please. It's fashion show time, and you're next up."

While Krista changed back into leggings and a sweater, Desz donned her white lace dress, which was the perfect foil for her dark skin. The jagged hem showed off her friend's toned legs to full advantage.

Like Krista had done only moments before, Desz studied herself in the mirror. She shook her head, her dark mass of corkscrew curls wafting, then falling back into place.

Satisfaction filled Desz's brown eyes. She smiled. "I clean up pretty darn good, if I do say so myself."

"You're beautiful." Krista glanced around the room. "What shoes are you wearing?"

"My glossy red Louboutins." Desz waved a hand. "Since this is a Christmas ball, I thought a pop of color was indicated."

"You thought right." Krista nodded her approval.

"The eyes of every man in that ballroom are going to pop when they see you walk in," Desz told her.

Krista couldn't stop the smile as she unzipped Desz's dress. She cared about only one man's reaction. "Back at 'cha. You rock that dress."

Desz responded with a Cheshire cat smile before her expression turned serious. "My uncle is super stoked about your business venture."

"I'm excited about it, too." Krista paused, then added, "And a little scared. This would take me, and maybe Dustin, in a totally new direction."

"When you lost out on the Shibusa account, it was obvious that your current career was changing." Desz stood to pull up her leggings, then shifted to face Krista. "In addition to being amazingly gorgeous, you're a smart, savvy businesswoman."

"I don't have a degree or—"

"Stop." Desz's hand shot up, palm out, and her eyes turned fierce. "Don't disparage yourself, not to me. I've watched you over the past three years. Sure, your agent gave you sound advice, but you never just blindly went along with what Merline or the powers that be suggested. You've got a good head on your shoulders. That and your strong work ethic are why you've been so successful."

For several seconds, Krista could only stare, touched to her very marrow by Desz's words. "Th-thank you."

"You and Dustin will make this new venture a success. Even if he changes his mind, you'll do it on your own and soar."

"Having him with me will make it all the sweeter."

"I think that's the way it's supposed to be," Desz said matter-of-factly, "when you're in love."

CHAPTER NINETEEN

Dustin tipped the deliveryman, then hung the tux, rented from a store in Burlington, in the closet. One more thing to mark off the list of Things That Must Be Done. Kenny had come through, not only getting Dustin a last-minute fitting yesterday, but persuading the shop owner to deliver the altered garment today.

Of course, it probably didn't hurt that Kenny had promised to give the business a nod of recognition in the Mistletoe Ball program.

Tomorrow night was the big event. The ball would mark the end of his and Krista's stints as *Hollywood Stars*.

With thoughts of his future bumping around in his head, Dustin had spent the past two days doing research. He'd revisited what he'd learned in college about business plans, considered funding options and upfront business costs. Once that was done, he'd made a list of possible locations. He'd then compiled a list of people in the industry who were possible resources.

After he and Krista spoke with Percy and Sondra, there would likely be more people to add and more lists to be made.

He wanted to know all there was to know about the industry he was considering jumping into with both feet. Though excited about the project, and energized by all he was learning, Dustin had to admit the thought of making such a major move had his stomach in knots.

Playing hockey had been his life, his dream for as far back as he could remember. Being on the ice here in Holly Pointe had brought back in full force just how much he loved it. Even the classes he'd taught had come easily, so coaching would be a natural transition. Would going in a completely different direction be a mistake?

Yet, the opportunity to do this kind of work with Krista excited him, too. Especially the thought of the two of them working closely day in and day out. He could easily see them building not only a career together, but a life together.

Dustin frowned, realizing he had yet to speak with her today. Though she was undoubtedly busy, he'd grown used to speaking —and texting—with her numerous times a day.

The ring of his phone brought a smile to his lips. She must be missing him as much as he was missing her. He answered without looking at the screen. "Hello, beautiful."

Silence filled the other end of the line for a heartbeat. Then a dry chuckle. "I can't recall the last time anyone called me that, but I appreciate the compliment."

Dustin recognized Coach Walenski's voice immediately. He stifled a groan. "Coach, I thought you were someone else."

"Obviously." Humor danced in the word. "How are you doing, Bellamy?"

For a second, Dustin pondered how to answer the question. "Good. And yourself?"

"Doing well." Coach paused for a second. "I was glad to see you back on the ice."

"Pardon?"

"I saw the film of you in some town in Vermont." Coach laughed. "Though the opposition left something to be desired, you looked good."

"Are you referring to the pond hockey game?"

"That's the one." The coach laughed again. "Looked like a lot of fun."

"It was." Dustin still wasn't sure why Walenski had called him. He decided the direct approach was best. "What can I do for you, Coach?"

"You can come back."

Dustin bobbled the phone, then regained control and tightened his grip. His heart began to beat an erratic rhythm. "The doctor's reports say—"

"They don't know everything." The coach's tone was dismissive. "Doctors wrote off Kong, and he came back and played three more seasons for us."

John Oterikong had been an outstanding defenseman before Dustin's time, but Dustin had heard the stories. In a single year, Kong had undergone surgeries on his right shoulder as well as both hips. Yet, he'd returned to the ice to help his team win their third Stanley Cup. The guy was a legend, a player who didn't know the meaning of the word *quit*.

"Kong was a beast."

"He was indeed." The admiration in Coach Walenski's voice came through loud and clear. "When we discussed you coming back, I said it was up to you. I should have been more encouraging. I know the kind of competitor you are."

"Hockey is my life." Dustin paused. "Or was. But I'm confused. Freddie led me to believe you didn't want me back."

"I don't know where he got that. Freddie's the one who thinks you should go in another direction. But Freddie is only looking at this from a business point of view. He wants you off the ice because he thinks it gives you more options in the long term. Maybe he's right on that." Coach paused. "But I know playing is in your blood. Are you really ready to call it quits?"

With great effort, Dustin kept his tone easy. "Freddie makes a strong case for coaching."

Coach made a dismissive sound. "You're not meant to coach. You're meant to play. Which is why you should come back."

Dustin dropped into the closest chair. "You read the medical reports. My ACL is garbage."

"I've read each and every one of those reports." The coach snorted. "None of them said you couldn't play, only that you likely wouldn't be at full speed."

"Dr. Wallace said it was more than that. I could end up being unable to skate at all."

"That's a worst-case scenario. His job is to tell you every possibility, I get that, but let's be real. Every player is always one hit away from that kind of injury. Your ACL may have taken a hit, sure, but your hard work in rehab paid off. The muscles that support your knee are in top shape."

"But—"

"Let me finish. You're one heckuva player and a fierce competitor. Even on a bad day, you're better than most of the players out there. That includes anyone we might bring in to replace you."

"That's nice of you to say."

"I'm not saying it to be nice, Bellamy. I'm keeping it real. We want you back. And don't give me any bullshit about not playing if you can't give a hundred and ten percent. I feel confident we'll get our money's worth out of you even at a hundred percent." Coach laughed. "You know what I mean."

"This is a surprise." Dustin found himself at an uncharacteristic loss for words.

"We've had other team specialists review your records, and they think you can play."

But at what cost?

The thought rose unbidden, and Dustin shoved it to the side. "You've given me a lot to think about."

"Don't think too long. We want you back. And we want you back yesterday."

When the call ended, the weight of the decision Dustin faced seemed even weightier. Though he knew Freddie would be supportive no matter what he decided, like Coach Walenski, his agent had his own thoughts.

But this was a decision that couldn't be made by committee. It was his life, Dustin told himself. The decision was his alone.

～

Krista slanted a sideways glance at Dustin and beamed. "This is so much fun."

"I'm glad you called."

The smile on Dustin's face didn't lessen Krista's unease. When she'd texted and asked if he wanted to come out and help her and Desz build a snowman, though he'd agreed immediately, she'd thought he sounded weird.

She figured he must be stressing about Freddie. Either he was having a hard time telling his agent about their plans or was dreading doing so.

Still, when he stepped out of his cabin, he'd embraced the task and had appeared to enjoy himself. When Desz had begged off, saying she needed to finish her blog, he'd joined Krista in razzing Desz about being all work and no play.

After patting snow on the tiny head of the snowman, Krista paused. "It feels as if this is the first free time I've had since I arrived. That isn't true, of course, but this trip to Holly Pointe has certainly been a whirlwind of activities."

Dustin scooped up another handful of snow. "You've enjoyed all of it."

"Every minute. I'm really happy." In fact, she couldn't keep from smiling. "And I'm looking forward to our future."

Krista noticed the sudden tight set to Dustin's jaw. Suddenly unsure, she pushed forward to fill the quiet. "I spoke with my parents today. And my brother and his family."

"How are they?"

"Doing well and excited about the new venture." Krista smoothed the snow across what would end up being the snowman's face. "They think it sounds like a great idea. Of course, they're apprehensive about me taking on the risk of a new business. But I told them, 'No risk, no gain.'"

"It is a risk," Dustin agreed. "Twenty percent of new businesses fail during the first two years, and forty-five percent fail during the first five."

Something in the way he relayed the stats had Krista turning to face him instead of picking up more snow. "Sounds like you've been having second thoughts." When he didn't answer, she prompted, "Are you having seconds thoughts?"

"I've simply been gathering information," he told her. "Just like what we'll be doing when we speak with Percy and Sondra."

"You're right. It's a huge undertaking. We need to be sure it's the right way to go." She offered him a smile. "For both of us."

He cleared his throat. "I just got off a call with Coach Walenski."

Her heart picked up speed. "He's the coach of your team?"

He nodded.

"Bet he wants you back." Despite her racing heart, Krista could have cheered when the words came out casual and offhand, just as she'd intended.

"He does." Dustin flung the snow in his gloved hands to the ground. "He had some other doctors read the reports. They think I can play."

The sudden pressure in Krista's chest made breathing difficult.

Better now than later, she told herself. She took a deep breath and willed her suddenly racing heart to slow. "I guess what matters is what you think."

He met her gaze head on. Gray eyes meeting blue. "I'm not certain I'm ready to give up the game."

Somehow, she managed to force a smile.

"I want to start this new venture with you, but the game is what I've lived for all these years." He blew out a breath. "I'm getting pressure from all directions. Freddie is pushing me to do one thing. Coach is pushing me to do another, and you're pushing me to go in a totally new direction."

Something in Krista snapped.

"Hold on a minute. I'm not *pushing* you to do anything. I told you my plan and invited you to consider joining me. You're the one who said you might be interested. If you no longer want to consider it, that's your choice. At this point, I don't have all the information to know if the plan is even viable." Krista took a deep, steadying breath. "If it turns out to be viable, I'll go ahead even if you decide to return to the team, so don't worry about me. Make the best decision for you."

"What about us?"

Her breaking heart had her throat clogging. Krista cleared it. "I think it would be difficult to keep a relationship going from such a distance. Especially with you focused on resuming your career and me busy launching a new one."

Shock filled his eyes. "Are you saying you're willing to walk away from everything we've been building?"

Krista's temper spurted. She held on to it with both hands and quelled the impulse to remind him she wasn't the one changing the plans. "I'm being realistic, Dustin. You already made it clear you can't do hockey and be in a relationship at the same time."

He blew out a breath.

The swash of red across his cheekbones told Krista she wasn't the only one fighting for control.

He spoke through gritted teeth. "By saying you can't be with me if I go back to the team, you're giving me an ultimatum—you or hockey."

"That isn't fair, and you know it." This time, Krista couldn't stop her voice from wobbling a little. "You've encouraged me to believe in myself, to see that I have it in me to start this new venture and be successful." When she continued, her voice was strong and steady. "Are you now saying that isn't true? That I shouldn't try so I can accommodate you instead?"

He whirled and strode to a tree, bracing both hands on the bark of the thick trunk.

His chest moved in and out, and her heart lurched. She wanted to tell him they could make this work. But she feared in the end they would both be hurt even more.

She moved to him and stroked his back with one hand in a soothing gesture. "It's not that I don't care. I do. I love you, Dustin."

The words popped out. She hadn't meant to voice her feelings. In fact, she feared that saying them in this moment would seem to him like emotional blackmail.

He turned, and she saw hope flash in his eyes.

Before he could speak, she placed the palm of her gloved hand against his cheek. "I realize we've never spoken of love. It seems way too early. But I know how I feel. I just want you to understand that walking away would be just as difficult for me."

When Dustin opened his mouth, she closed his lips with her fingers.

"If we're meant to be together, I truly believe we'll find each other again." The tight squeeze in the area of her heart made speaking difficult, but she pushed forward. "In the meantime, we'll live our lives and move forward with our own dreams."

Dustin pulled her close, and she rested her head against his jacket front.

"Where do we go from here?" His voice was gravelly and rough.

Hadn't he heard what she'd just said? Then Krista realized he was talking about the immediate future.

"We finish our time as *Holly*wood Stars." Tears welled, but she blinked them back as she spoke to the front of his coat. "We'll go to the Mistletoe Ball. We'll dance and laugh and enjoy every minute of what will be our last night together."

"Last night," he repeated, then cleared his throat. "That has such a final ring."

"If it's meant to be, we'll find each other again," she repeated and forced a little laugh. "Let's just hope it doesn't take another ten years."

CHAPTER TWENTY

Krista kept her emotions in check until she was safely inside the cabin. Once the door shut behind her, she headed for the sofa. Collapsing onto the cushions, she hugged a pillow tight against her aching heart and let the tears fall.

"I'm sorry I had to—" Desz stopped at the edge of the living room. "Omigod, what happened? Are you okay?"

Krista could only shake her head.

At her side in seconds, Desz dropped down beside her and simply wrapped her arms around her. Clinging to her, Krista cried until she could cry no more.

Then she straightened and swiped at her eyes, offering Desz a watery smile. "Sorry. I don't usually cry like this."

Desz's dark eyes searched hers. "You never cry like this."

Lifting one shoulder, Krista sniffled. "I don't know what got into me."

It was a silly thing to say, since she knew very well what had gotten into her. The love of her life no longer wanted to be with her. Tears welled at the realization, but this time, Krista blinked them back.

"Want to tell me what's going on?" Desz's voice was as soft as a caress.

Krista knew Desz wouldn't press if she said she didn't want to talk about it, but she wanted—no, needed to share. She only hoped doing so would lessen the pain. "Dustin has decided, well, practically decided, that he's going back to Canada to play hockey."

"Wait. What?" Confusion furrowed Desz's brow. "I thought his injury—"

"Apparently, other doctors disagree with the specialists and say if he wants to play, he can." Krista blinked rapidly. "Hockey is what he loves."

"He's backing out on your deal. Just like that, with no warning." Desz's eyes flashed. "That—"

"We were simply exploring the option of working together, Desz." Krista placed a staying hand on Desz's arm when her friend began pushing to her feet. "Nothing was decided."

"The heck it wasn't." Desz's lips pressed together. "It's a bad choice."

Krista studied Desz. She was lucky to have such a wonderful, supportive friend. "You may see it as a bad choice, but it's his to make. I can still launch my own busi—"

"I'm not talking about hockey. I'm talking about you."

"Me?"

"Look at you, Krista. A few weeks ago, you were lost over where your career would go. Then you show up here and, in a matter of days, come up with ideas that have helped revitalize this place."

"I—"

Desz held up a hand. "Please, let me finish. You came up with a whole new career plan for yourself. You opened yourself up to another person the way you never have before and are even willing to let him go, putting his happiness above your own.

Everything on that list takes courage. Any man who can walk away from a woman like that will live to regret it."

Krista considered everything Desz had said and thought of Dustin. Would she ever get to the point where she'd be able to look back on this time and think simply that she was glad they'd briefly reconnected? Or would the memories of him have her forever yearning for a happiness that had once seemed within reach?

"Thank you, Desz. For your kind words and for your support. It means the world to me."

"I'm with you, girl. One thousand percent."

Expelling a ragged breath, Krista massaged her temples.

Concern furrowed Desz's brow. "Are you okay?"

"I've got a headache. Too much crying." Krista fought for a light tone, but couldn't quite pull it off. "I'm going to lie down and rest for a few minutes. Hopefully, I can stop it before it really gets going."

Desz gave an understanding nod. "Is there anything I can do?"

"There is one thing you could do." *Coward*, the tiny voice inside Krista whispered. "Would you mind texting Dustin to tell him you and I will meet him at the ball tomorrow night instead of riding together?"

Desz nodded. "I'm happy to do it."

Krista stood, and when her friend rose, Krista hugged her, giving her an extra squeeze before stepping away. "You're a good friend."

Desz's dark eyes searched Krista's for what felt like an eternity, as if she were seeing deep into her soul. "You deserve the best. Don't ever settle for less than you deserve."

"Thanks again."

Desz's words circled in Krista's head as she entered her bedroom, closed the door and dropped down on the bed.

Don't ever settle for less than you deserve.

It was as if Desz had been speaking to her situation with Dustin as well as with the modeling agency.

For years, she'd given the industry her all and had been rewarded. Now she would be going out on top. While it might not be important to other models, she'd come to understand that it was important to her.

Dustin… Well, she knew she'd never be content with a long-distance relationship. With several-times-a-week phone calls and texts. With occasional visits over holidays. With never fully being a part of his life.

In the end, their relationship would disintegrate and leave them both brokenhearted.

As she was drifting off to sleep, it struck Krista that when she'd told Dustin she loved him, he hadn't said it back.

Dustin paced the small living room as the moose above the mantel stared at him. At one time, he'd been firmly convinced that his decision to attend college, rather than be drafted straight out of high school, was the most monumental decision he'd ever make. Now, he faced an even bigger one.

Dustin expelled a ragged breath, recalling Krista's words. She loved him. He'd wanted so badly to say the words back to her, but how could he tell her in one breath that he loved her and in the next that he might be returning to Canada? That wouldn't make sense. Of course, neither did walking away from the woman he loved.

Yet, hockey had been his life for—

A knock at his door had Dustin's heart slamming against his rib cage. *Krista.* Coming to tell him…what? That they could try to make long-distance work?

He jerked open the door, hoping to see her on the porch.

Instead of Krista, Desz stood, gazing at him with an inscrutable expression.

"Hi." As he stepped aside to let her in, he did a quick visual sweep of the porch.

"If you're looking for Krista, she isn't with me." Desz's normally upbeat persona was gone. Dark eyes searched his. "She asked me to let you know we're going to drive separately tomorrow night. She said I could text you, but I thought it'd be easier to just stop over and tell you myself."

"Why didn't she tell me?"

Desz shrugged. "She has a headache and is lying down."

That didn't explain why she couldn't just contact him later. Unless she'd already started pulling back. Though the thought sliced his heart, it was no more than he deserved.

Jamming his hands into his pockets, Dustin rocked back on his heels. "Is she okay?"

Desz cocked her head, her tone decidedly cool and just a little belligerent. "What do you think?"

"I think I need a beer." Dustin shifted from one foot to the other. "You want one?"

After hesitating for a long moment, Desz nodded. "Okay."

Dustin grabbed two beers. When he found Desz still standing, he gestured to the sitting area. "Make yourself comfortable."

"It's hard to be comfortable with that moose shooting daggers at me." Despite the comment, Desz took a seat in one of the chairs.

"Krista doesn't like him either." Just saying her name brought a fresh stab of pain—and a realization.

Desz took a long drink from the bottle he'd handed her, her gaze sharp and assessing.

Dropping into the chair opposite hers, Dustin expelled a long breath. "Remember when you asked if you could interview me about finding my passion for your blog?"

"I remember." She lowered the bottle. "You said no."

"I said not then."

"Are you ready to do the interview now? Is that what you're saying?"

"Not now." Dustin leaned forward, resting his forearms on his thighs. "But our conversation got me thinking how hockey has been my passion since I was a kid. I lived and breathed it. In my head, I knew there would come a day when my career would be over. I wasn't certain what I'd do when that happened. I guess I hoped I'd find another passion and the right woman and move into the second phase of my life."

"Now you found the right woman, but it's not the right time." Desz's dark eyes searched his. "Or maybe Krista isn't the right woman."

Dustin ignored the comment. "I'm getting pressure to go back on the ice. A month ago, I'd have been willing to take the risk of screwing up my knee permanently for a chance to play again. The sport was all I had in my life."

"Hockey is your passion." Desz's tone was matter-of-fact. "I get it."

"That was part of my dilemma, but not all. I don't want to lose Krista. I can't lose her." Dustin nearly told Desz he loved Krista, but swallowed the admission. Krista needed to be the first to hear the words from him. "She means everything to me."

"That wasn't the impression she got this afternoon."

"When I spoke with Krista, I'd just gotten off a call with Coach Walenski. I was thinking out loud, and then everything escalated too fast. By the time I had a handle on the situation, Krista was essentially breaking up with me."

"She thinks you're going back to Canada to play." Desz inclined her head. "Are you?"

Dustin stayed silent and stared at his beer.

"Dustin? Are. You. Going. Back?"

"I need your help, Desz."

"No. What you need is to tell me what is going on, because if you think I'm going to help you when you've left my best friend in tears—"

"I'm going to make it right, I swear. I know what I want now. I've got a plan. First, I need to call my agent. Then, I need your help."

CHAPTER TWENTY-ONE

The second Krista pulled to a stop behind several cars in line for valet parking at the Barns of Grace Hollow, Desz pulled out the phone she'd dropped into her purse only minutes ago, her thumbs flying.

"Who'd you text?" Krista asked.

"Lucy." Placing her phone onto her lap, Desz leaned forward, checking her lipstick in the vanity mirror. "She plans to take you around to a separate entrance. That way, she can position you and Dustin for your grand entrance. I can't wait to see you walk the red carpet."

Krista inched the car forward and waited while the people in the luxury sedan in front of the Subaru got out. "If that's the case, why aren't we parking by that entrance? And why is Lucy texting you and not me?"

"I was texting her about a blog idea earlier and said I'd pass on the message. Anyway, don't worry about it." Desz snapped the cover on the vanity mirror shut. This is your final duty as a *Holly*wood Star. Are you sorry to see it end?"

"I've had a blast." Krista's lips curved in a slow smile. "I've fallen in love with Holly Pointe all over again."

"You'll come back." Desz spoke with utmost confidence. "Who knows? You may even have a home here someday."

"Maybe," Krista agreed, though she wasn't sure she could return to Holly Pointe without seeing Dustin everywhere. Though perhaps with time…

A hand on her arm had Krista jerking her gaze in Desz's direction.

"Are you okay?" Desz asked.

"Just a little melancholy." Krista suppressed a sigh. "Endings are difficult."

Desz squeezed her arm. "This is just the beginning."

As soon as they stepped out of the car, Lucy strode over to greet them.

"The place looks amazing." Krista breathed the words, craning her neck back and unable to keep from staring. The barns were gorgeous enough on their own, but the beauty of them festooned in white lights and greenery stole her breath.

"Wait until you see the ballroom." Lucy turned to Desz. "You look a-ma-zing."

"Thanks." Desz beamed. "You're hot enough to scorch."

Lucy wore a simple blue velvet gown with a collared vee neckline. Though relatively demure by anyone's standards, the look was incredibly sexy on Lucy.

"Thanks." Lucy glanced at Krista, then back to Desz. "Do you mind if I steal your friend?"

"Long as you give her back," Desz said.

"Promise." Lucy chuckled. "Check out the side room before the dancing gets started. There's lots of wonderful silent-auction items. And remember your ticket to the Mistletoe Ball includes all the food you want as well as two tickets for complimentary drinks."

"Stellar." Desz's face brightened. "See ya later, *Holly*wood Star."

While Desz entered through the front entrance, Lucy

escorted Krista around to another door and then down a long hall to a VIP area.

"Dustin is already here," Lucy told her. "You two will have a few minutes, so just relax and enjoy. I'll come get you both once most of the guests have arrived. Kenny is going for the big splash."

"Most have seen us before," Krista reminded Lucy.

"Not everyone. And certainly not in all your finery." Lucy gestured with one graceful hand to the dress. "The dress is gorgeous on you."

"One More Time gets the credit."

"Dustin is in there." Lucy pointed to a door, then frowned as her phone literally squawked.

Krista jumped. "What kind of ringtone is that?"

"Chicken." Lucy smiled. "With all the noise, I needed something guaranteed to get my attention." Lucy read the text and blew out a breath. "Issue with the band." She turned to Krista. "You're okay?"

"Absolutely."

"I'll take care of this, then be back to get you both when it's time."

"Thanks for all you've done, Lucy. You're a wonder."

"Just doing my job."

"Well, I can easily see you running this whole operation one day." Krista chuckled. "Heck, I can see you running the town."

"Stranger things." Lucy patted Krista's shoulder. "Gotta run. Stay in the room until I return to get you."

Lucy was already out of sight by the time Krista squared her shoulders and opened the door.

Dustin stood at the window, staring out into the darkness.

He turned as she walked in.

"I'd know that perfume anywhere."

To her discerning gaze, his smile appeared forced.

Krista pretended to sniff the air. "Ditto."

"You look amazing." Starting at her feet, his gaze moved slowly upward. "Better than amazing."

"You don't look too shabby yourself." Dustin in a hockey jersey or a flannel shirt was one thing. In black tie, well, he was magnificent.

He flashed a smile. "Hardly a ringing endorsement, but I'll take it."

"How've you been?" Considering she'd just seen him yesterday, it was a silly question. But since arriving in Holly Pointe, they'd spent so much time together that not seeing him last night and today had seemed like forever.

"Lonely." He took a step forward. "I've missed you."

When he took another step, she held up her hand. "Please. Don't. This is hard enough."

"You do realize that not only will we be walking down the red carpet arm in arm, but we'll be expected to spend most of the night dancing together." He rocked back on his heels and blew out a breath. "That makes it sound like a chore, when nothing could be further from the truth. I want to enjoy the evening with you."

"I don't know how I'm going to get through this," Krista admitted. "Knowing that after tonight—"

"Let's enjoy the evening." Dustin's tone turned persuasive, but it was the pleading look in his eyes that touched her heart.

"You mean pretend?"

"It won't be pretending. Don't you see?" He'd moved forward. Though he stood close enough to touch, his hands remained at his sides. "I want to spend this time with you. I think you want to spend it with me."

Krista hesitated.

"We'll embrace the day, or rather, the night." This time, he did reach out and took her cold fingers in his. He brought them to his lips for a kiss, never taking his eyes off her face. "Please, Krista."

All that's guaranteed is now.

She wasn't sure why that saying popped into her head, other than it fit this situation perfectly.

Tomorrow she would say good-bye to Dustin. But tonight he was hers.

Krista lifted her chin, met his searching gaze. "Let's do it."

The clock struck eight. The red carpet was rolled out.

Krista waited with Dustin for the Christmas processional music to begin.

She might have walked more runways than she could count, but never had Krista's heart hammered so hard. She took several calming breaths.

She felt Dustin reach over and take her hand.

When she turned to him, he smiled. "We've got this."

"Yes." She returned his smile. "We do."

Then the signal came, and they began to walk. She wasn't sure if Dustin meant to keep holding her hand. All Krista knew was she wouldn't be the first to let go.

As Lucy had instructed, they took their time strolling down the endless aisle of red. They waved to the crowd with their free hands and scattered smiles as cameras flashed.

When Dustin slanted a glance at her and smiled, Krista's answering smile came easy. This was their night. They'd earned it.

Only when they reached the raised stage where the band sat and Kenny stepped between them did Dustin release his hold.

Taking each of their hands in his, Kenny lifted them high. "Let's hear it for our fabulous *Holly*wood Stars."

The crowd roared their thanks and approval.

"Remember to check out the silent-auction items in the other room." Kenny's deep voice boomed. "The items were all donated, and every penny of the money raised will go toward funding local health programs."

More applause and cheers rang out.

"We're almost ready for our stars to open the dance floor," Kenny announced. "But before they do, Dustin Bellamy has asked to say a few words."

As Kenny drew Krista off to one side, Dustin moved to the microphone.

"Thank you, Kenny and Lucy, for giving me this opportunity to speak from the heart." Dustin's gaze swept the crowd, then returned to briefly settle on Krista before returning to the audience.

"This time in Holly Pointe has been special to me for so many reasons. I believe that a life without passion is no life at all. For most of my life I've had only one—hockey."

Conscious of the gazes directed her way, Krista kept a smile on her lips and her chin up.

"As many of you know, I suffered an injury that many thought would end my career. To my surprise, it hasn't. In fact, my coach called yesterday and urged me to come back. There is nothing that could have surprised me more than getting this news."

Applause broke out in the ballroom, but Dustin motioned the crowd silent.

"Regardless, I've decided to hang up my skates."

Krista inhaled sharply, as did most of the crowd.

Dustin turned to face her. "Yesterday, I called my agent and my coach and told them I'm officially stepping away from hockey. It's time for a new career."

Krista was sure she'd misunderstood. Her heart beat so loudly in her ears, it drowned almost everything out.

She kept her eyes on Dustin as he turned back to the crowd.

"Since coming to Holly Pointe, I've discovered a new passion —Krista Ankrom." His smoky gray eyes returned to her. "Not just her beauty, but her beautiful mind. Her creativity and kind, generous spirit have inspired me to want more out of life. I want a life with a house and a yard, maybe a dog. But more than anything, I want a life with Krista, the woman I love."

Tears stung the backs of Krista's eyes, but she didn't let them fall. Not even when Lucy took her arm and guided her to where Dustin stood.

Dustin held out his hand, and when she grasped it, he dropped to one knee.

"I love you, Krista. Hockey is my past, but you're my future." His voice grew husky, and he paused to clear his throat. "You're my soul mate, my everything, the love of my life. My heart is, and always will be, yours."

Krista blinked rapidly, but didn't—couldn't—take her eyes off Dustin. Her heart began to sing. If this was a dream, she didn't want to wake up.

"I want us to build a new and wonderful life where we work and play together. I want to grow old with you." He gave her hand a squeeze, and the love in his eyes burned hot and bright. "Krista, will you marry me?"

"Yes," she said in a small voice that shook with emotion. Then, in case he hadn't heard, she spoke again in a louder voice. "Yes. Oh, yes."

He rose and grinned. "I don't have a ring. I thought we could pick one out together and—"

"I don't need a ring." She flung her arms around his neck and lifted her face for a kiss. "All I need is you."

A great cheer rose up as his mouth closed over hers, signaling the start of their new and wonderful life together.

EPILOGUE

SIX MONTHS LATER

A Southern Girl in NYC
Blog Post

The wedding of supermodel Krista Ankrom and NHL hockey star Dustin Bellamy took place on Saturday, June 11, at the Barns at Grace Hollow in Holly Pointe, Vermont.

The rings the couple exchanged were custom-made by a local designer. Ms. Ankrom's dress, a gorgeous fit and flare with pearl and crystal beading, was designed by Madeline Tomes, an up-and-coming NYC fashion designer and friend of Ms. Ankrom.

The couple are skipping a honeymoon at present to go straight to Tennessee for the premiere of their new TV show, *Down Home with Dustin & Krista.*

Now, for the best part. Yours truly was maid of honor, and I have the up close and personal pictures and details you won't find anywhere else…

∾

I hope you enjoyed visiting Holly Pointe and experiencing all the wonder of the holidays while seeing Dustin and Krista fall in love under the falling snow.

The next book in this heartwarming holiday series brings us back to Holly Pointe ten years later. A lot has changed but the joy of Christmas shines through in Holly Pointe & Mistletoe. You'll also get to see Dustin and Krista and catch up on what's been happening with them.

Embrace the magic of Christmas by grabbing your copy of Holly Pointe & Mistletoe or read on for a sneak peek:

SNEAK PEEK OF HOLLY POINTE &
MISTLETOE

Chapter One

Eight days ago Stella Carpenter swore off caffeine. This morning
she instructed the barista to add a second shot of espresso to the
grande coffee she ordered.

She'd quit because she didn't like being dependent on
anything. Or anyone. Excluding, of course, her good friend
Tasha, on whose couch she was currently crashing every night.

Shifting impatiently from one foot to the other, Stella pulled
out her phone. She had time to wait. Being summoned to your
former boss's office demanded a little liquid courage.

The middle-aged man behind the counter held up a cup and
cast a glance in her direction. "Stella."

Until she'd been reduced in force from the *Miami Sun Times*
three months ago, Stella had visited this particular freestanding
kiosk daily. Eduardo had been a barista at this stand since she'd
started her job two years earlier.

"It's good to see you again." His voice was as warm as the
morning sun. "Are you working out of the office today?"

Her heart lurched as she lifted the cup from his hand. "Just came in for a meeting."

Stella stuffed a bill into the tip jar, then headed in the direction of the beautiful art deco building housing the *Miami Sun Times*.

Even though it was nine a.m. and almost Thanksgiving, heat already rose from the sidewalk, and the hairs on the back of her neck were moist. In southern Florida, there was no hoping for snow on Christmas. When her parents had relocated the family to Miami when she was in her teens, she'd quickly discovered that hot and sunny was the forecast no matter what the time of year.

Stella's heels clicked on the glittering sidewalk as she entered the building that housed the city's largest newspaper. For the past two years, she'd been a reporter and—in a pinch—a photographer and videographer.

Now her job and those of many she'd worked with were gone, replaced by freelancers.

Cool air rushed over her as she crossed the marble floor to the security station. Once cleared, she took the ornate bronze-decorated elevator to the office of Jane Myers, the newspaper's managing editor. The early-morning text from Jane had sent Stella's hopes soaring.

Freelancing had fallen short of paying her bills. It was at times like this that Stella wished her parents hadn't put her inheritance in a trust she couldn't touch until she turned thirty.

She'd been lucky her lease was up. Her first action had been to let her apartment go. The past three months, she'd been bunking on Tasha's couch.

Tasha's roommate had started to grumble about another person in their small apartment. Last week Tasha had brought down the hammer, telling her she needed to be out by the first of the year. Stella understood, though she wasn't sure where she would go.

Thankfully, she had over a month to figure it out.

When the elevator doors opened onto the fifth floor, Stella stepped out and paused for a long drink of the steaming coffee.

Larissa, Jane's personal assistant, barely gave Stella time to push back her perspiration-dampened hair before ushering her into Jane's office.

Her boss's dark-brown hair was pulled back into a severe chignon. The pale-blue eyes Jane fixed on Stella were firm and direct. The red "cheaters" hanging by an eyeglass chain around her neck added a bit of whimsy, but there was nothing whimsical about Jane's no-nonsense gaze.

"Thank you for coming in on such short notice." Jane rounded the desk. Her stern expression softened infinitesimally.

Stella relaxed when Jane finally smiled but didn't let down her guard. "I was surprised to hear from you."

Jane leaned against her desk as if trying to ease the formal air of the meeting.

"It's been a while since we've talked." Jane inclined her head. "Do you have plans for Christmas?"

Whatever the reason for this unexpected meeting with the newspaper's managing editor, Stella knew it wasn't to discuss holiday plans. She found it odd that Jane was asking about Christmas when they'd yet to get through Thanksgiving. "No plans. I'm hoping to pick up a freelance job or two."

Something flickered in Jane's eyes, an emotion Stella couldn't interpret. Another woman might have launched into a speech about a balanced life. Those words would never make it past Jane's lips. No one was more of a workaholic than her former boss.

Stella inclined her head. "What about you?"

"I plan to have a few friends over. An eclectic group of Miami's movers and shakers. These men and women know where all the bodies are buried. Figuratively speaking, of course. I'm hoping to dig up some juicy kernels."

The comment didn't surprise Stella. Last year Jane had been brought in to shore up the *Sun Times*' bottom line. Immediately after her arrival, the paper began focusing on sensationalized news instead of serious, multisource journalism.

Stella hadn't liked the switch. She would always be grateful she'd been able to work for several newspapers that valued high-quality journalism.

To be fair, the *Miami Sun Times* wasn't the only paper doing what it could to set itself apart. Most were doing all they could to attract readers and increase sales.

"So, Stella. You said you're looking to pick up more freelance jobs before the holidays. Does that mean work has been slow?"

Her assessment caught Stella off guard, as did her expression, which struck Stella as something between concerned sibling and hungry wolf. "Well, no, not exactly—"

"Because I know how hard freelancing can be. Especially with *so many* journalists competing for work."

Hm, Stella thought, *wolf it is.*

"I have an assignment for you." Jane straightened, her tone all business. "It will involve travel and approximately six weeks away from Miami. All expenses will be covered."

Before Stella could comment or ask any questions, Jane continued. "If the end product meets with my satisfaction, there may be a staff position available for you starting the first of the year."

Stella kept her expression impassive despite the urge to jump up and do a happy dance. A chance to be back on staff was a dream come true. She'd spent the past three months sending out resumes all over the country but had yet to receive a single bite. "I'm intrigued. Tell me more."

Jane gestured to the guest chair before rounding the large modern desk to sit behind it, formalizing the interaction. Her boss folded her long, elegant fingers and rested them on the shiny onyx.

"Holly Pointe, Vermont, was recently recognized as the Christmas capital of the USA. Not just commercially, the people have been rated as the kindest in the country. The 'capital of Christmas kindness.'" Jane's sarcastic tone told Stella just what she thought of the honor. "I'm interested in doing a feature on the town."

Stella experienced a surge of excitement. This could be fun. Since her parents had passed away, holidays had been especially lonely times. Tasha was spending Christmas with her family in Jacksonville. She'd invited Stella to come along, but she'd gone the previous year and had felt like a fifth wheel. "I love heart-warming features, especially at holiday time."

"I don't believe you understand." Jane leaned forward, her eyes cool and assessing. "I'm not interested in heartwarming fluff. Positivity doesn't sell nearly as well as drama. I want an exposé of the town's underbelly. Whatever dirt there is, I wanted it dug up and in my inbox by December 24."

Stella hesitated. An infinitesimal second, but enough for Jane's eyes to turn to ice.

"I'm trying to help you, Stella, so I offered this to you first. But if this isn't your cup of tea, it's no problem. Juliet is also interested in coming back full time. I'm sure she'd be happy to take this on if you pass."

Though Jane offered no promises, Stella knew that if she delivered, she'd get her job back. Something told her that if she didn't—or if she turned down this assignment—she could also kiss any freelance work good-bye.

"I won't disappoint you." Stella met Jane's steady gaze. "When do I start?"

Light the fire, get a nice cozy blanket and dive into this beautiful, touching novel.

Holly Pointe & Mistletoe

ALSO BY CINDY KIRK

Good Hope Series

The Good Hope series is a must-read for those who love stories that uplift and bring a smile to your face.

Check out the entire Good Hope series here

Hazel Green Series

These heartwarming stories, set in the tight-knit community of Hazel Green, are sure to move you, uplift you, inspire and delight you. Enjoy uplifting romances that will keep you turning the page!

Check out the entire Hazel Green series here

Holly Pointe Series

Readers say "If you are looking for a festive, romantic read this Christmas, these are the books for you."

Check out the entire Holly Pointe series here

Jackson Hole Series

Heartwarming and uplifting stories set in beautiful Jackson Hole, Wyoming.

Check out the entire Jackson Hole series here

Silver Creek Series

Engaging and heartfelt romances centered around two powerful families whose fortunes were forged in the Colorado silver mines.

Check out the entire Silver Creek series here

Made in United States
Orlando, FL
20 September 2022

22605116R00124